MIMOSA FORTUNE

ECHO FREER

Hodder
Children's
Books

A division of Hachette Children's Books

Acknowledgements: I am extremely grateful to the following people for giving me so much help when I was researching this book: Christiane Kroebel of the Whitby Archive and Heritage Centre, Whitby; the staff at Whitby Museum & Art Gallery; Whitby Literary and Philosophical Society; the staff at the Captain Cook Memorial Museum, Whitby; the staff at Saltburn Smugglers' Heritage Centre, Saltburn; Professor Robert Shoemaker, professor of eighteenth-century history at Sheffield University; Jamie McLaughlin, Humanities Research Institute, Sheffield University; Patricia Labistour of Robin Hood's Bay, author of *A Keg of Good Brandy* and *A Rum Do*. I am also grateful for the Internet and the many websites that offered me a wealth of information about legal proceedings in the eighteenth century, in particular www.oldbaileyonline.org. I would also like to thank the office staff at Whitby Community College, and stress that none of the characters in this book is based on anyone from the college – Heaven forbid! Thank you to Kameran Dhillon for allowing me to use his name. And finally, I want to thank my husband, Frank, and my children, Imogen, Verien and Jacob for being there for me.

Text copyright © 2007 Echo Freer

ablished in Great Britain in 2007 by Hodder Children's Books

he right of Echo Freer to be identified as the Author of is Work has been asserted by her in accordance with the Copyright, Designs and Patents Act 1988.

1

ISBN-13: 978 0 340 89476 7

Typeset in Baskerville by Avon DataSet Ltd, Bidford-on-Avon, Warks

Printed in the UK by CPI Bookmarque, Croydon, CR0 4TD

The paper and board used in this paperback by Hodder Children's Books are natural recyclable products made from wood grown in sustainable forests. The manufacturing processes conform to the environmental regulations of the country of origin.

Hodder Children's Books
a division of Hachette Children's Books
338 Euston Road, London NW1 3BH
An Hachette Livre UK company

For Magic Mo, with love

1

You know the worst thing about talking to spirits? They never tell you what you want to hear – well, not the really important stuff anyway. For a start, it would be quite nice to know next week's winning lottery numbers. I don't mean so that I could win for myself – spirits never tell you things for selfish reasons, that's one thing I *have* learned. But imagine how many starving children and homeless people I could help if I won!

Or what would have been really useful was if the spirits had given us a hint that the guy sitting across the crystal ball from Wanda and me was a member of the Dutch underworld, trying to locate some hidden loot through the spirit of his recently deceased brother. I mean, don't get me wrong, I'm not asking for a thunderbolt to blast through the ceiling, but I think a subtle hint along the lines of, 'Hey, you might think he's been working his pecs down the gym but, actually, he's packing a shoulder holster under his jacket,' wouldn't have gone amiss.

But that was obviously too much to ask, so there we were again, Wanda and me, doing a runner with the Amsterdam Mob in hot pursuit. And, to be honest (which, of course, I almost always am), I'm fed up with running. If the Universe had meant me to be a runner, it would've given me sneakers for feet.

Wanda's my mum, by the way. She hates being called Mom, or Mother, or any of those older generational sort of names. She says it makes her feel old. Well, hello! Wake up and read the tea leaves! Not that she's ancient or anything – in fact, Wanda's quite cool really. But talk about Wanda by name, wander by nature! Over the past fourteen years I've probably lived in more places than most people could even name, but never for very long and there's usually a string of irate locals on our tails when we leave. We've done all the conventional escape routes, like planes, trains and the odd 'borrowed' automobile – plus more than a few unconventional ones, such as the time we had to be rolled up in a carpet to dodge a pretty furious hotel owner in Istanbul.

On this occasion though, Wanda had surpassed herself; she'd fluttered her eyelashes and managed to get us free passage – travelling zillionth-class,

scrunched up under some very smelly lobster pots
– on a boat that was smuggling booze from the
Hook of Holland to Whitby in Yorkshire!

'What a nice man! His name's Teddy,' she
whispered. She was smiling in the direction
of a burly man in a sou'wester. 'I'm getting a
good feeling about Whitby.' She was trying
simultaneously to wave at Teddy and untangle the
sequins of her headscarf from where they'd got
trapped in the mesh of a lobster pot.

Personally speaking, I wasn't getting a good
feeling about anything at that moment. In
fact, lying curled up under half a tonne of smelly
fishing gear with leg cramps, seasickness and the
meanest-looking crustacean I've ever seen giving
me the evils, the only feeling I was getting
was nausea.

'Yes, I think this is going to be a good place to
make a new start,' Wanda continued, tucking her
hair back into her scarf. 'And of course, they'll
speak English, so you can go to school again.'

'Great.' I must admit I wasn't totally over the
moon about that. Don't get me wrong; I love
learning. I've always got my head in a book – when
Wanda doesn't want me to assist at a sitting or help
her with the cooking or something. It's just that all

that formal education stuff's a bit of a waste of time if you ask me. Last time I was in school we were in Barbados and, I'm not being funny, but who needs pythagorisms, or whatever they're called? And as for all that sport! But, with any luck, Wanda would upset the punters and we'd be out of England again in a couple of months – preferably somewhere hot – so I wasn't going to lose sleep over a bit of schooling.

Famous last words! Did I say I wasn't going to lose sleep over a bit of schooling? Well, rewind!

I managed to put off enrolling at college for a while, partly because it was the Easter holidays when we arrived and partly because we were getting settled in to our new cottage. It seems that for once, Wanda's instinct had been right and Teddy, the trawlerman who'd let us stow away in his hold, really had taken a shine to her. And, even better than the free passage across the North Sea (what could be *worse*?) was that he owns a holiday cottage that he wants to let out, and he said that we could live there rent-free! The only condition was that we decorate the place for him. Wanda always says, 'There's no point in worrying about the future, sweetie, because the Universe always provides.' And, you know what – she's never been wrong yet!

I reckoned it would take Wanda a good few months to earn enough money even to buy the paint, so I felt fairly sure that we'd be here for a while – clientele permitting! After years of squatting in condemned caravans and derelict barges, what a relief it would be to stay put – in a proper house, with a proper bed, a proper flushing toilet and a roof that didn't think it was a colander. And, as an added bonus, it was really pretty too.

Whitby goes back hundreds of years and the Old Town has narrow cobbled streets with lots of little yards behind them. There could be half a dozen fishermen's cottages in each yard, some of them built on top of one another, and our cottage was one of those. It was down a little alley that led to a small beach at the mouth of the harbour, and it had stone steps up to it with pots of geraniums all the way to the front door. But the best bit was, my bedroom looked right out over the harbour, which meant I had the most amazing view of the sunset. I loved it and, to be honest, I was thinking that I wouldn't mind if we did settle here for a while.

Or so I thought! But the minute the schools went back, Wanda and I found ourselves standing in front of a woman who was built like a nuclear fallout shelter. And boy, was she giving Wanda a grilling about my education – or lack of it. Oh my days! If ever an aura was in need of cleansing, it was Miss Basham's.

'And why has Mimosa been out of full-time education for over a year, Mrs Fortune?' She was speaking to Wanda as though she'd just crawled out from under a very slimy stone.

'Oh, she hasn't, and call me Wanda, please.'

Miss Basham sniffed like she'd just trodden in something ucky. 'So kindly explain her lack of formal schooling, *Mrs Fortune*.' Uh oh! If she knew Wanda, she so wouldn't emphasise the *Mrs* part.

'I've been educating her at home.' Wanda was smiling, but it was one of those smiles that had about a zillion volts behind it. 'And, as I said, I am *Wanda* Fortune. I've nothing against men but I've never felt the need to attach myself to one and I have no need for a title. My marital status is no one's business but my own . . .' She looked over Miss Basham's shoulder to where a load of certificates were hanging on the wall and added, '. . . Euphemia.'

Miss Basham was standing arms akimbo like a Sumo wrestler in tweed and Wanda was squaring up to her. It looked like they were both cruising for a bruising, so I thought it would be best if I stepped in before things started to turn ugly.

'So anyway, have you got a place for me, or shall I carry on learning at home?' I tried to keep it light. 'No pressure – I'm easy either way.'

And that's how I ended up in GCSE Science the next morning. The teacher was OK – young and pretty cool. He did his best to make me feel welcome. 'Now, Mimosa, I don't know how much of the syllabus you've covered in your last school . . .'

'Oh, none,' I said fairly confidently.

He looked a bit weird at that but he carried on anyway. 'At the moment we're discussing renewable energy . . .'

'Brilliant,' I said, because if there's one thing I know masses about, it's energy.

He looked a bit happier. 'Would you like to tell us what you know?'

Would I? 'OK, well, Reiki is renewable energy for a start.' I noticed the guy was looking a bit confused. 'I mean, it comes straight from the Universe and the Universe is infinite, right?' His eyes were screwed up, like he didn't understand what I was talking about. 'And instead of draining the healer it actually energises the person giving the Reiki, so, in a way, Reiki is the ultimate renewable energy.' I thought I'd acquitted myself pretty well to say it was my first day. Then I added, 'I was the youngest Reiki Master ever when I was attuned.'

'That's ... er ... interesting, Mimosa. But we were actually discussing geothermal energy and its impact on the environment.'

Whoops! But that was cool too. 'Oh, I know masses about that as well. I used to live right next to a geothermal spa when I was in Iceland and, come to think of it, when we lived in Japan too. And, actually, we lived rough in Yellowstone National Park for a while when I was a baby, not far from Old Faithful, that massive geyser. But I don't really remember that very well – not without being regressed, anyway.'

I looked round and everyone in the class was staring at me – I was thinking, maybe I shouldn't have shown off with the whole youngest Reiki Master thing. Oh well, what the heck! As Wanda always says, 'Let your light shine, sweetie, and you'll give other people permission to let theirs shine too.'

There was only one boy in the whole class who

wasn't gawping at me like I'd just been beamed down from the mother ship. Kameran, his name was, and he was smiling at me in this really friendly way – not flirty or anything, just really sweet. I don't often stick around long enough to do the making-friends thing, so I smiled back. They always say that boys and girls can't be friends because the whole *lurve* thing gets in the way, but I don't think that's true. Although, to be honest, I wasn't really sure how friendships worked. But I was getting a nice energy from Kameran, so I was up for giving it a go.

2

I knew my first instinct about education was right! Talk about regimented! I was expected to dress up in a uniform that made me look exactly like everyone else. In loads of the schools I've been to students have been allowed a bit of creativity and personal expression in their clothes, but not here! I hate uniforms, they're so militaristic and they suck the flair and individuality out of anyone – but that's just me having my little soap-box moment!

There'd also been a couple of sticky incidents with the teachers in the first week. In English, Mrs Mitchell asked us to write an essay on *To Kill a Mocking Bird* – but my argument, that it's never acceptable to take the life of another living creature, didn't seem to be what she had in mind. I ended up doing a detention – which actually didn't turn out so bad because she said I had to use it to familiarise myself with the book. A whole hour to sit and read! You see, the Universe knows what it's doing.

Plus, Wanda had acquired an old bike for me to

get around on, but college was at the top of this whacking great big hill and there was no way I was going to cycle up that. In fact it'd taken me so long to push it up there, I'd been late every day and had ended up having an unpleasant encounter of the military junta kind with Miss Basham. So, all in all, I was relieved when it was Friday. And I'd been really looking forward to the downhill ride after school. I'd even bought a couple of those kiddies' windmills to stick in the basket on the front so that they'd spin round as I went whizzing along.

'Hey, Mimosa! Wait!' It was Kameran calling after me.

He'd been really sweet all week. Two girls in my tutor group, Milly and Amanpreet, had been assigned to showing me round and Kameran had asked if he could join them. So I'd got to know him a little bit but even so, I was surprised to see him running across the grass towards me. He was still in his basketball kit and a group of girls by the wall were practically dribbling as he ran past them.

'Hi,' he said to me. 'Do you mind if I walk with you?'

What a dilemma − the chance to build a friendship or five minutes of free-flow exhilaration? 'Oh, I'm sorry,' I said. 'Normally, I'd say yes, but I have a hill to freewheel down.' He looked a bit disappointed, so I added, 'But maybe we could walk halfway.'

'Thanks,' he smiled. 'Hey, listen – Milly Ventress says that you told them in RE that you can read tarots. Is that true?'

'Of course it's true!' I was a bit cheesed off that he had to even ask. I mean, why would I lie about it? Especially the way that old fossil Miss Devine practically had one of those appo-plastic fits, or whatever they're called. 'The occult! The occult!' she started wailing, the minute I got out my cards. 'I will not tolerate devil worship in my lessons.' I did tell her that she needn't have worried because I don't believe in any sort of worship, but that just seemed to make her worse. Two girls had to carry her out to the medical room to recover. Anyway, Miss Basham thinks it's probably best if I don't take RE as one of my options now, which is fine by me – if option is supposed to mean choice, then it wasn't one of *my* options anyway. In fact this whole going to school thing is definitely not my option at all, but there you go!

'Would you read my tarots?' Kameran asked.

Phew, what a relief – at last, someone who was

open-minded. 'Sure. I charge thirty euros for a full reading but I could do you a short one for ten.'

He did a quick calculation then said, 'That's about six pounds seventy-one pence. Will you do it for a fiver?'

Hmmm! Nice negotiation. I grew up bartering in the bazaars of Marrakech – until Wanda and I had to make a hasty exit across the desert on camels one night – so I was impressed with Kameran's easy bargaining. 'Six pounds, to stay as near to the original price as possible, but I'm rounding it down to keep the math simple,' I replied.

He grinned at me. 'A fiver for me and I'll drum up more clients in school and you can charge them six quid apiece?'

Quite the entrepreneur! 'Done!' And we shook hands.

'Excellent! Can I come round tonight?'

I wrote the address of our cottage on a page in his rough book, and by the time Kameran came round, I'd persuaded Wanda to let me use the front room for the reading. She'd designated it to be her 'parlour' but she didn't have any clients that night. Anyway, it was so rare for me to have people round, I think she was secretly relieved that I seemed to be doing 'normal' teenage stuff. And I must admit, it was nice to have someone I could call a friend.

'Cool sneakers,' I said when he arrived, but he looked at me as though I'd just said something in a foreign language. 'Your sneakers.' I pointed to his footwear. 'I like them.'

'Oh – my trainers,' he corrected. 'Thanks.'

Pardon me for not speaking the Queen's English! I thought – but I didn't say anything. I beckoned him inside. 'Come through and take your jacket off.'

I'd lit the fire and drawn the curtains in the parlour so that it looked really cosy. And I thought I'd got everything prepared but, when we sat down, my tarot cards weren't there. Which was weird, because I distinctly remembered placing them in the middle of the table before I answered the door.

'Hold on a sec,' I said, leaving Kameran alone.

Wanda was baking muffins in the kitchen. 'You haven't seen my tarots, have you?' I didn't have to ask if she'd moved them – Wanda knows better than anyone that you never touch another person's cards.

'I thought you'd taken them into the parlour,' she said through a veil of flour.

Hmm! So did I! 'Never mind, I'll just have to use my astrological ones.'

But when I got to my room, the strange thing was, the little carved Burmese box that I keep my runes and tarots and everything like that in was wide open – and both my packs of cards were sitting right in the middle of my bed! I was sure I'd only taken out my regular pack.

I did a mental replay – open box, take out cards, close box, go downstairs. Nope – nowhere in my memory banks was there the tiniest recollection of putting both packs on my bed. Oh well – maybe I was losing my marbles as well as my tarots? Which is a little bit worrying because Wanda told me that Grandma Goodfox (that's my grandmother on my father's side) ended up in an institution for the criminally insane – something to do with a pickaxe and an obsession with the cable guy. But Wanda's almost certain it's not hereditary.

Just let it go, I told myself, giving my head a little shake – it's just a few collywobbles because this is your first reading in a new town. And, of course, it's always more nerve-racking when you're working with a friend – if Kameran counted as a friend after only a few days. I wasn't sure.

And when I got back to the parlour, I started to

think that maybe he *didn't* count as a friend, because he seemed to have done a runner on me. I was three hundred per cent positive I'd left him sitting at the table when I'd gone off card hunting and yet, hey presto, here he was – gone! Hmm! Now, forgetting where you've put your cards is one thing, but forgetting where you put your client is way more worrying!

'Kameran?' I made a mental note to ask Wanda for more facts about Grandma Goodfox and the warning signs of insanity.

'Yes, sorry,' said a voice from behind the old armchair next to the fireplace. 'I'm here.'

I peered over the back of the chair and saw Kameran, huddled in his coat, crouched down practically *in* the fire. He was way too old to be playing hide-and-seek, so unless he was a secret pyromaniac, I guessed he might have been searching for a lost contact lens or something like that.

'I got a bit cold,' he explained, standing up and moving over to the table. 'OK if I keep my jacket on?'

'Fine,' I replied. And, I must say, as I crossed the room I was starting to feel a bit chilly myself. 'I'll put another log on the fire.' I picked up one of the lumps of wood from the basket next to the hearth, but before I could put it into the flames, a huge black cloud of smoke billowed out of the fireplace.

Kameran leaped back. 'Whoa!'

'Soot belch,' I said, fanning away the smoke. 'It means the wind's in the wrong direction.'

'It wasn't windy when I was coming here. It's probably the chimney that needs sweeping,' he suggested as he coughed his way out of the smog and sat down at the table.

I shook my head. 'No, it was almost the first thing Wanda did last week. She's very particular about chimneys – ever since the one where we were staying in Canada caught fire and burned down the whole log cabin.'

Kameran smiled. 'Is there anywhere you *haven't* lived?'

I shrugged. 'Oh, loads of places, I expect. Now, shall we get started?'

I picked up the tarots, but no sooner had I begun unwrapping the silk scarf that I keep them in than something else strange happened: the curtains started flapping about. At first it was just a gentle flutter, but then they whooshed right out into the room. It was like there was a hurricane blowing outside. Oh boy! For my first reading in a new town, this was not going according to plan at all.

But Kameran seemed to find the whole thing funny. 'Oh, I get it – these are all part of the special effects, right? You know, mysterious things happening to create a creepy atmosphere. I expect your mum's hiding in a broom cupboard somewhere and, any minute now, she'll be knocking three times pretending to be some long-lost auntie from the other side.'

I must say, I was disappointed in him. I'd thought Kameran had been genuine when he'd asked me to read his cards, but now he was taking the baklava like everyone else.

I gave him one of my *looks* – Wanda says they'd scare the bejezzus out of Old Nick himself. 'This isn't Hollywood, you know. Tarots should never be treated lightly. If you're not serious there's no point in going on.'

He held up both hands in a gesture of submission. 'Sorry, it was just all the stuff with the fire and the curtains and everything.'

'Like I said, it's the wind, OK?'

He cocked his head on one side and smiled. 'I guess I've just been watching too many scary movies, eh?'

'Something like that,' I said, shuffling the cards.

'Now, is there anything in particular that you want to know the answer to? Or is it just a general reading you're after?'

'Well . . .' Kameran lowered his eyes and looked embarrassed. 'There's someone that I really fancy and I want to know if it's likely to go anywhere.'

'OK.' I gave a little shudder. Even though the fire was roaring, the room was feeling icier than a freezer in Antarctica. I reached over for Wanda's shawl that she'd left over the back of the chair and wrapped it round my shoulders before carrying on. I handed the cards to Kameran to shuffle too, but I could see that he was shivering so much his hands were shaking.

When he'd finished I spread out the cards on the chenille tablecloth and asked him to pick out five cards with his left hand. As I turned them over, I looked at the cards in front of me: they were nearly all from one suit.

'Oh wow!' I exclaimed. 'So many cups! Including the ace! Boy, are you in for some serious love!'

He looked at me sheepishly and grinned. 'Cheers! It's been worth my fiver just to hear that.'

I went through the meaning of each card with him and, as I was explaining the reading, it occurred to me that I was pretty sure I knew who it was he fancied. If I were a betting person, I'd have put my bottom euro on it being Milly Ventress, the girl who's been showing me round. That's obviously why he'd been hanging around with us all week. And I had an amazing idea – how fantastic would it be if I could get them together, as a sort of thank you to them both for being so kind to me? Oh wow, that would be so brilliant. I always think it's good to have a project on the go and Kameran and Milly were going to be mine – for as long as it took Wanda to get us evicted from Whitby, anyway.

I was feeling quite excited about my new goal and was just standing up to let Kameran out when there was another blast of wind and the metal latch on the door began to rattle as though someone was trying to come in.

'It's probably just Wanda,' I explained. Then I called, 'It's OK. You can come in now. We're finished.' But when I opened the door, Wanda wasn't there. She wasn't even nearby because I could hear her chanting in the back room. How bizarre!

And at that minute, there was a crash from over by the window. I looked down and saw the pot plant that Teddy had placed on the windowsill for Wanda lying in a mess of terracotta and soil on the floor.

'You got a cat?' Kameran asked.

I shook my head, puzzled. Then the curtains blew right out into the middle of the room again, till they were almost at right angles to the floor. Ah, that explained it!

'Boy, do we need to get some industrial strength draught excluder in this place!' I said to Kameran.

He gave me a sideways look. 'You sure your mum's not hiding behind there with a hairdryer?' But the minute he'd said it he held up his hands again. 'Just kidding!'

I walked him to the front door and, as he left, he told me that he'd put the word about and get me some more readings – which was a relief. It'd been such a strange evening, it wouldn't have surprised me if he'd never wanted to have anything to do with me or my tarots again.

'Night,' I said, waving him off down the steps. 'See you at school on Monday. And mind the geraniums.'

I watched him walk down the alley towards Church Street. At the bottom of the steps, he turned to wave back at me, slipped off his jacket and tossed it over his shoulder. 'It's warmer out here than it is inside,' he called as he broke into a jog and disappeared from view.

He was right: it *was* mild. And not a breath of wind, either. Weird!

3

True to his word, by lunch time on Monday, Kameran had lined up three clients for me at six pounds a time. Brilliant! If I could keep this up, Wanda and I would have the cottage decorated in no time.

I wasn't totally happy about the venue he'd found for our little enterprise, though. I like to try and create a degree of spirituality when I do a reading, but the store cupboard at the back of the gym had about as much spirituality as a launderette on a wet Saturday night in Vladivostok. And believe me, I should know!

'I tried everywhere,' he said apologetically. 'The RE room, the Year 12 common room, the library. This was the only place that would guarantee privacy.'

'It's cool,' I said, forcing a smile on to my face to try and combat the smell of sweat from the PE group who'd just been in there. The fragrance didn't have quite the same ambience as the incense and rosewater I usually use, but I didn't want

Kameran to think I was ungrateful. To make things even more uncomfortable, the store cupboard was right next to the boiler room, so it was like an oven in there and the heat made the sweaty smell even more pungent. 'Really, it's fine. I've done readings in worse places.' Which wasn't strictly true. Even though I believe that honesty is absolutely the best policy, I like to think of the truth as a bit like a band-aid – it sometimes needs to be stretched to cover up the wound and make people feel better. Kameran wasn't looking totally convinced, so I sat myself down on a pile of rubber mats, used the leg of the vaulting horse for a backrest and grabbed a large plastic storage box of shuttlecocks for a table.

'See – perfect!' I reassured him.

Kameran was still looking dubious, but he took up his position outside the door, doubling as lookout and cashier.

First up was a sixth-former called Celia Winterbottom who wanted guidance on whether or not to take a year out after her exams. The message in the cards was that, instead of worrying about what to do *after* her exams, Celia would have been better if she'd worked harder *before* them! I didn't tell her that, though – best not to give people bad news. So I told her that she was about to embark on a period of learning and hard work – I left it up to her to decide whether that would be at university, crammer-college doing resits, or backpacking round the world attending the University of Life.

Then came Kameran's friend Joel, who was about as convincing a client as an Inuit would be a desert scout. I didn't need to be psychic to see that Kameran had put him up to it.

'So what would you like guidance on?' I asked, spreading the cards on the plastic box of shuttlecocks.

Joel was trying so hard not to laugh that there was nearly a puddle on the mat.

'You tell me – you're the one who's supposed to read minds.'

Wow – that's original!

I gave Joel a general reading, and was shocked to see that, for someone who always seemed to be joking about, there was masses of sadness in his past. And, I didn't tell Joel this, but his future didn't look too promising either. In fact, I couldn't see anything beyond his twenties. To be honest, it kind of spooked me a bit, so I didn't say anything except to hand him his money back and tell him to go out and treat himself to something nice.

'Wow! I like this – Kameran pays me to come and have my fortune told and you do it for nothing. At this rate, I'll be worth a mint. Cheers!' he laughed, stuffing the money into his pocket as he left.

I never like it when a reading shows something unpleasant but, as a professional, I mustn't let it affect me. So I gathered myself for the final client, Milly, the girl who'd been showing me round. All last week Milly had been going on and on about her new boyfriend, Eddy Proudfoot. Only now, she'd heard a rumour that he was cheating on her. She wanted to know if it was true and, if so, what to do about it. I was tempted to give her her money back and just tell her to dump the skunk, but when I looked at her cards, I realised this was the perfect opportunity to kill three birds with one stone – I could guide Milly towards a more reliable romance, put my matchmaking skills into action *and* assist my new friend Kameran in his pursuit of love. I felt very excited.

'I see new beginnings and romantic changes,' I told Milly. 'Look out for someone of a loyal and faithful nature . . .'

'Sounds like a golden retriever,' Milly commented, rubbing her arms and giving a shiver. 'Ooo, it's gone cold in here.'

She was right, the cupboard had suddenly gone from furnace to freezer in about a nanosecond. I pulled my own jumper round my shoulders and carried on. 'No, this is definitely *not* someone of the canine variety – and romance is *very* well aspected.' My plan was going way better than I'd hoped. I studied the cards again and saw just what I was looking for. 'He's tall, athletic, intelligent . . . human!' I added, just to be sure she wasn't going to go out and buy a puppy. 'It's someone already close to you . . . and I see the letter K.'

Milly would need to be severely intellectually challenged not to realise that the cards were pointing her in the direction of Kameran. Everything seemed to be going brilliantly, when I heard a strange rumbling – not loud enough for an earthquake but definitely louder than a late lunch. I stopped. It seemed to be coming from just above our heads.

Then there was a faint knocking on the door.

'Aaaagh!' Milly almost jumped out of her skin. Her eyes were the size of dinner plates and all the blood had drained from her face. Kameran's head appeared round the door. 'You idiot!' she said to him. 'I thought you were a—'

'Sssh!' he whispered. 'There's someone in the girls' changing room. Keep out of sight.'

He took a step forward to join us in the cupboard, but just at that moment the source of the overhead rumbling was revealed: a row of volleyballs had inexplicably started trundling along the shelf above us, picking up speed until they began rolling off the edge – just over the door. As the first one fell, it hit Kameran right on the crown of his head. He reeled forwards and fell into the cupboard with a groan. Other balls bounced down, hitting the box of shuttlecocks and sending my tarots flying into the air. One ball ricocheted off the edge of the box, hit a trampette then bounced off the trampette and knocked over a stack of badminton racquets that cascaded to the floor with a clatter. Another ball crashed into a pile of cones that were used to practise dribbling, while a third smashed into a box of table-tennis equipment so that the volleyballs were joined by half a dozen of their smaller, ping-pong cousins, all raining down on us in a pretty spectacular ball-fest.

The whole episode probably only lasted ten seconds, and when the activity finally stopped, Kameran sat up looking dazed.

'There is something seriously spooky going

on whenever you use those cards,' he said, rubbing his head.

I was beginning to think he was right. This was only the second time I'd done readings since we'd arrived in Whitby and both times weird things had happened. I looked up to the ceiling and said, to no one in particular, 'Listen, if you guys don't want me doing this stuff, then you only have to say. You don't need to wreck the place.'

The colour that had only recently returned to Milly's cheeks drained from them again. 'Stop it – you're scaring me.'

'If anyone's going to be doing any scaring, it'll be me!' a voice boomed from the other end of the gym. 'Come out of there immediately!' Even from inside the storeroom I could tell it was Mrs Twigg, the PE teacher. I'd only encountered her once before (and that was through a badminton net when I'd been trying to discuss the merits of non-competitive sport) but I'd decided that if ever there was an argument for *not* saving the whales, it was Mrs Twigg. Now, get me right – my love of exercise doesn't extend much beyond yoga and nature walks, but even *I* could see that Mrs Twigg had to be the worst advert for PE – ever! Not only was she the size of your average beluga, but also, whenever she opened the door to her little room, a mushroom cloud of smoke escaped into the changing rooms. A girl could die of passive smoking just putting on her tracksuit. Come to think of it, that's probably why she'd snuck in there that lunch time.

'Come here,' she bellowed. 'THIS MINUTE!' Whoa! She really needed to address her anger issues.

Kameran and Milly went straight across to where she was waiting at the other end of the gym, but I needed to gather my tarots, so I stayed in the store cupboard. From the ranting and raving going on, I was getting the impression that Mrs Twigg was unaware of me and thought that Kameran and Milly had been on some sort of clandestine love tryst – which shows that I'm not the only one who thinks they'd make the perfect couple.

I counted up and realised that I was still one card missing. Looking round, I caught sight of it peeking out from under a table-tennis bat. But as I reached down to pick it up, I could've sworn I heard someone whisper something. I stood up and listened. There it was again: a male voice. And he sounded close. Hmm! Strange! I hoped no one had sneaked into the cupboard and overheard what I'd been saying to my clients.

'Come out,' I whispered. 'Whoever you are.' Mrs

Twigg was still giving Kameran and Milly the benefit of her barbed-wire vocals and I did have a twinge of conscience that I wasn't out there with them taking my share of the blame, but it was crucial that I got all my cards first, so I kept my voice down. 'I know you're in here.'

I looked around, but the number of hiding places in the cupboard was pretty limited. I peered behind the plastic football goals and took a peek inside the wooden vaulting box, but there was definitely no one in there. I decided it was probably the caretaker in the boiler room next door. From the subzero temperature, I assumed that the boilers must have broken down, so there was probably some pretty frantic maintenance work going on next door. Feeling relieved that client confidentiality hadn't been breached, I bent down and picked up the last card. Hmm, interesting! It was the Hanged Man.

Personally, I don't believe in coincidence. I am a firm believer in synchronicity: everything happening at a specific time for a specific reason. So, I wondered, what did it signify that this card was the last one to be found? Bearing in mind that the Hanged Man shows the need to adapt to change (like I haven't done *that* all my life!) and to make adjustments and sacrifices in order to move on (don't even start with the things I've had to sacrifice every time we've upped sticks and done a runner), was this telling me that I was going to have to give up my blossoming friendships and move on again? Already? I hoped not.

I was just about to give myself up and face the wrath of Mrs Twigg, when I heard the voice again – only clearer this time.

'T'Anged Man!' it said, urgently. 'That's what Ah need ti talk ti thi aboot.'

Oh my days! There *was* someone in the cupboard with me. And he seemed to be talking in a foreign language.

'I don't know who you are, but you shouldn't be in here,' I said, trying to sound cross – in a whispery sort of way. 'Readings are supposed to be private!' I had no idea where he was hiding, so I looked up in the vague direction of the shelf that the volleyballs had been on.

'Is there someone else in there?' Mrs Twigg had obviously heard him too. 'Come out immediately.'

'You heard her,' I said under my voice. 'She wants you to go out there – immediately.'

'Ah know tha canst 'ear me, so tha must listen,' the voice said. And then it dawned on me – he wasn't speaking in some little-known Scandinavian dialect, as I'd previously thought – it was actually English. But, oh boy, what weird English! Understanding some of the kids in college was hard enough, but this was like the Whitby accent – and some! I strained my ears and concentrated as he went on, 'A great wrong's bin done. In t'year of our Lord seventeen 'undred and fifty-four, a man wor 'anged as shouldn't 'ave bin. Tha *must* help us!'

I froze. Oh boy! This was either a very elaborate practical joke, or . . . no, I wasn't even going to go there. But before I could go anywhere:

'YOU AGAIN!'

Uh oh – I'd inadvertently positioned myself in the door of the storeroom, and the smog zone that was Mrs Twigg had spotted me. She'd diverted her fury from Kameran and poor Milly (who was almost in tears) and was now bearing down on me from the other end of the gym.

Great – from ghost to ghoul in one minute – my day was just getting better and better. I looked from the cupboard to the gym, where the enormous Mrs T was thundering towards me, and back to the cupboard.

'I don't know who you are, but back off,'

I muttered, as the lumbering PE teacher loomed closer.

'Who do you think you're telling to back off?' she boomed.

Which was absolutely *not* what I'd intended. I wasn't sure how I was going to get out of this one.

I poked my head out of the door and tried to disarm her with a smile. She had an expression like a rampaging rhino, so I guessed I probably needed to work on my disarmament strategy.

'Er . . . no one,' I called, looking round the storeroom, frantically searching for anything that might let me off the hook. 'I was just saying . . .' Suddenly, like an answer to a prayer, an old shelving unit toppled over on to the mats. 'I was just saying that I needed to get this *rack* off.' Phew! Talk about a narrow escape. 'It's fallen on my foot.'

Then, moving away from the door, I whispered to the voice, 'If that was your doing, I'm very grateful but please leave me alone. I can't help you.'

With that, I walked out of the freezing cupboard and into the swelteringly hot gym, to meet my fate.

4

Whenever something nasty happens to me, I've developed this brilliant technique of switching off and singing songs in my head. So while Mrs T was giving me an earbashing, I was mentally singing an old Bolivian nursery rhyme that (roughly translated) is the Latin American equivalent of, *Wibble wobble, wibble wobble, jelly on the plate.* I'd like to think that the fact that it came into my head at that particular time had nothing whatsoever to do with Mrs Twigg's bouncing quadruple chins but as I said before, I don't believe in coincidence.

I was up to my eighth rendition when she finally wound down. 'So, all three of you will have an hour's detention tomorrow. Meet me outside the Sports Hall after last lesson where you can begin repainting all the hockey balls.'

Milly's bottom lip began to pucker and she looked really teary. 'Mam'll go mad. I've never had a detention before.'

I felt terrible; this was all my fault. Although, when I thought about it, maybe not *all* my fault –

Kameran ought to take some responsibility. After all, it was his idea in the first place. And he did select the storeroom as the venue.

'I've never had one either,' he said, putting a consoling arm round Milly's shoulder. Then he grinned. 'It's kinda cool.'

Yes! I did a mental victory punch to see them getting up close and personal. It's so satisfying to see people's readings coming true. As for the detention, I wasn't sure about it being cool – that's probably just a macho boy thing – but I can't say it was bothering me that much either. Painting hockey balls for an hour was a perfect opportunity to practise my mediation.

A couple of things were really getting up my nose, though. The first was the whole hearing voices incident. I hadn't said anything to the others because it had freaked me out a bit. It's one thing to get intuitive messages through the cards, but to have a spirit actually *speak* to you is a whole different crystal ball game. Even though Wanda sometimes says she's seeing or hearing spirits, between you and me, I'm not totally convinced – and neither are most of her clients!

The other thing that was bugging me was the fact that Mrs Twigg had taken my cards. Tarots are extremely personal things and I certainly didn't want her energy contaminating my best set. And it didn't help that, when I got home, Wanda was being ridiculously parental about the whole thing.

'Sweetie, you've only been there a week and you've been given two detentions, had to drop a subject and now your livelihood's been confiscated. What's happening to you? I think that school's having a negative effect on your aura.'

OK, so maybe *ridiculously parental* is a slight exaggeration, but believe me, for Wanda that was harsh.

'It's *not* having a negative effect on me.' We were setting up the parlour for Wanda's evening sitting and I'd just put a match to the fire. 'I like it at college. I have friends there.' I was just getting the hang of this 'making friends' thing, so the last thing I wanted was for Wanda to take me out of school again.

'OK then, sweetie. But I don't want you turning into some juvenile delinquent,' she warned, as she placed her crystal ball on the table and straightened the tablecloth.

'I'll try harder,' I agreed. I hardly thought that doing a few readings in my lunch break was going to earn me an ASBO.

When Wanda does sittings, it's my job to create the atmosphere in the room. I'd already lit the tea light under the little urn-shaped burner with rose oil in it, and placed an aromatic joss stick by the door. And I'd just taken another match and was going round the parlour lighting the candles, when I noticed my hand was trembling. Whoa! This was ridiculous. How could I possibly be feeling nervous about a sitting? I'd helped Wanda hundreds of time and I'd never felt like this.

And then it dawned on me: when I'd looked up to the storeroom ceiling and told the spirits that if they didn't want me doing this stuff, they only had to say, I really hadn't been prepared for them actually to respond from beyond. It was a huge career leap to go from simple psychic to mystic medium in a single lunch break and I still hadn't got my head round it. But to make matters worse, I hadn't told Wanda. To say that I'd been sparing with the truth was an understatement. I'd owned up about the illicit tarot readings, but what I'd omitted was the fairly crucial matter of having a spirit speak to me. I don't know why but every time I tried to tell her, something stopped me. And I hate holding things back from her. Wanda and I have never had secrets.

Oh well, here goes, I thought. If I say it quickly before the client arrives, then it'll all be over and done with. I took a deep breath. 'There is something I need to talk to you about.'

Wanda obviously hadn't picked up on the urgency in my voice because she was going through a pile of sequined headscarves, holding each one up to the light.

'Mmm?' she queried, holding a turquoise one with Turkish coins sewn round the edge against her lilac top. 'Does this one go, sweetie?'

'The purple one would be better.' I placed an enormous floor-standing candlestick by the wall and drew the curtains. 'Wanda, something happened today.'

But just then the ship's bell that hung over the front door clanged loudly and I jumped. We've lived here over two weeks now but that bell still frightens the bejeebers out of me every time it's rung.

'I'll have to tell Teddy to do something about that,' Wanda said, tying the turquoise scarf round her head and pushing the last wisps of hair up inside it. Then she giggled, 'It's loud enough to wake the dead!'

I didn't know if I'd been saved by the bell or

beaten by it, but either way I decided to forget the whole hearing voices episode and just hope that it was a one-off and things would settle down to normal again. If Wanda wanted to go down the mediumship route, that was up to her; I was just going to stick with my intuition.

And speaking of intuition, the moment the client walked in, my intuition told me that tonight was going to be interesting – and I don't mean that in a good way. She had wild, badly permed hair, fuchsia lipstick randomly smeared round the bottom of her face and narrow piggy eyes. She was wearing a brown skirt, grey blouse and a long green cardigan with a belt tied round her waist. I've seen better dressed sacks of rice! Normally I try not to judge a person by their clothes. After all, when Wanda and I lived in Mongolia, there were times when we had nothing to wear but animal skins. But even then, I like to think that we wore them with a certain panache. But this woman wouldn't know panache if it crept up and crimped her hemline.

'This is my daughter, Mimosa,' Wanda introduced. 'She'll be assisting me this evening.' She indicated for the woman to go into the parlour.

I held out my hand to shake hers but she

stomped past me, thrusting her bosom in front of her like a weapon of mass destruction.

'Aye, my lad's told me about her and her goings-on up at the college,' she said.

Wanda caught my eye and winked reassuringly. I winked back at her – or tried to. I've never been able to master the art of winking; I always end up shutting both eyes and looking as though I've got some sort of nervous disorder.

'Mimosa,' she said, 'this is Eva Proudfoot.'

'*Mrs* Proudfoot, if you don't mind. I don't hold with all this first names malarkey. Now just get on with it, will you?'

Proudfoot? I didn't need to be a genealogist to realise that this woman was somehow related to Milly's two-timing boyfriend, Eddy. I'd never met Eddy, but if the cards were to be believed (which of course they always are), then he was a majorly not-nice guy. And by the looks of things his mother wasn't much better.

Wanda indicated for Mrs Proudfoot to take her seat at the far side of the table. Wanda sat opposite and I switched off the lights and sat on a chair by the door, positioning myself so that I was behind Wanda but could see the client clearly. My role was to keep an eye on proceedings and tap Wanda on the shoulder if I saw that the client was in any way distressed or anxious.

Wanda placed her hands flat on the table either side of the crystal ball, dropped her head back, closed her eyes and took a deep breath through her nose. There was silence apart from the crackling of the fire in the inglenook and the mewing of seagulls outside. I love watching Wanda work and felt a tingle of excitement run down my spine. But then:

'You can cut out all that rubbish,' barked Mrs Proudfoot. 'I've not come here for theatricals. Just get on wi' t'job.'

Uh oh! That was definitely not a good start. Wanda's head snapped forward again and she opened her eyes. But she stayed very calm.

'Believe me, Mrs Proudfoot, I am not an actor. I was merely centring myself and preparing to open a portal to the other side.' The sequins on her headscarf twinkled in the candlelight. 'Now if you would be so kind as to allow me to continue.'

'I've never heard 'owt so daft,' continued Mrs Proudfoot. 'I used to go to old Freda Frickley over in Baytown and she never did any of this airy-fairy nonsense.'

Wanda smiled and inclined her head slightly but

I knew there was a volcano waiting to erupt inside her. 'If you want to cancel your appointment, Mrs Proudfoot, I would be happy to refund your fee. Minus the non-refundable deposit, of course.'

'Like heck I want to cancel it. I've come here apurpose, so don't think you can get out of it that easy!'

Without replying, Wanda closed her eyes and drew a deep breath again. This time she wrapped her hands around the crystal ball and began to mutter faintly as she lowered her head to gaze into the crystal.

'What was that, my darling?' she said softly to no one in particular. 'Have you got a name for me?'

'By, this place is a bit pokey, in't it?' Eva Proudfoot interjected. 'I'm all but on fire, I'm so close to the hearth. I'm used to more comfortable surroundings than this.'

'OK, that's it!' Wanda said, unwinding her headscarf and allowing her hair to cascade down her back. 'I'm sorry but I cannot work—'

At that moment all the candles in the room flickered and I gave a shiver as the temperature plummeted. Oh no! It was happening again.

'I see – more of your little dramatic effects!' Evil

Eva's head was nodding, in an I'm-on-to-you sort of way.

And then I heard it – the voice again. Not whispering this time – it was as loud as if he was standing next to me. 'Tell 'er that 'er mother says to go 'ome an' stop 'er caterwauling. She couldn't be trusted wi' t'money. That's why she didn't leave 'er owt.'

My eyes shot from one end of the room to the other, looking for a sign that either Wanda or Mrs Proudfoot had heard him too. But they both seemed totally oblivious.

'You're nowt but a charlatan.' Mrs Proudfoot was pushing her chair back and standing up. 'I'm off and I'll have my money back – all of it!'

'Fine by me,' Wanda was saying.

'Tell 'er. Now! Afore she goes,' the voice said to me.

Yeah, right! That would ease the tension, passing on a message like that to a woman who's already breathing fire and brimstone. I was looking round the room but I couldn't tell which direction it was coming from. 'Just go away and leave me alone,' I whispered.

I was suddenly aware that both Wanda and Eva were staring at me.

'Who are you telling to go away?' Mrs Proudfoot sounded indignant. Then, as she realised I hadn't been speaking to her, she folded her arms across her pendulous bosom and threw back her head. 'Oh, I see what's going on. Well, spare me any more of this poppycock! You must think I was born yesterday.'

'Tell 'er quick,' the voice said again.

'All right,' I said quietly. I looked Mrs Proudfoot in the eye and repeated the message I'd been given.

Wanda sucked in her breath. Evil Eva said nothing for a few moments. Then she slumped on to the chair, sitting down so heavily that a less sturdy piece of furniture would've crumpled under the pressure. She narrowed her eyes even more, so that they became like tiny laser beams boring into me. 'Has our Eddy been priming you, young lady?'

'I've never met Eddy,' I said. 'It was a message from the other side.'

'Oh really?' They always say sarcasm is the lowest form of wit, but there was nothing witty about Mrs Proudfoot.

Even Wanda sounded incredulous. 'Really?'

'Yes, really,' I told Wanda. 'That's what I wanted to talk to you about.'

Mrs Proudfoot was not convinced. 'Listen, I'm

not so green as cabbage looking, you know. The whole of Whitby knows my mother was a wealthy woman and she left the lot to a dogs' home. I haven't paid good money to hear the sort of information you could've got from any Tom, Dick or Harry. Now when I used to go to Freda Frickley . . .'

'Ah'm ovver 'ere,' the voice said. 'Canst tha see mi?'

My head was twisting and turning, peering into every nook and cranny to find the source of the voice.

'Our Eddy said your girl was soft in the head,' Mrs Proudfoot said, nodding in my direction. 'Look at her now. You should have her seen to.'

I was ignoring her by mentally singing 'Alice the Camel' as I strained my eyes against the candlelight. And then I saw him! There, behind Mrs Proudfoot, in the corner at the back of the room, was a boy. And oh boy, *what* a boy!

I gasped. 'Oh my God!'

'Mimosa?' I was vaguely aware of Wanda tapping me on the arm, but I was transfixed; this guy was seriously gorgeous.

Wow! Either the sexiest burglar in Britain had snuck into our front room or this was the physical manifestation of the voice I'd been talking to. It was a toss-up which was the better option; in view of his rugged good looks, I had a personal preference for the burglar, simply on the grounds that he would've been alive. But, unfortunately, all the evidence was pointing to the spirit scenario. Apart from the flickering candles, the subzero temperature and the unmistakable voice, there were his clothes. He was wearing a jacket that flared out from the waist, with a frilly cravat type of thing hanging round his neck and knee-length breeches. To be honest, he looked like a scruffy ancestor of Austin Powers. But what really clinched it was the merest suggestion of wallpaper showing through him. I don't know about you, but I don't know any living people who have that degree of transparency – well, not on a physical level anyway.

'Tha canst see mi canst tha?' he said, suddenly smiling. Whoa! My tummy did a back flip. He was leaning against the wall with his arms folded and one leg crossed over the other, looking so hunky I was finding it hard to remember he was only an apparition. 'Mi name's Quill – Quill Newton.' He bent forwards in the slightest suggestion of a bow and it was time for some internal gymnastics again.

'Ah can't tell thi 'ow relieved Ah am. Ah've bin tryin' ti get folk ti see mi for two 'undred-odd year.'

What was I supposed to do? I could hardly just say, oh really, that's interesting. I've never had a conversation with a ghost before and I wasn't sure I wanted to have one now, particularly not in front of Wanda and Mrs Proudfoot – who was still rambling on about what a fraud Wanda was. Which, sadly, I was beginning to realise might not be too far from the truth. And yet I was intrigued. OK – I admit it, my intrigue could have had something to do with the fact that he was so drop-dead gorgeous – if you'll pardon the pun! (Ghost, drop-dead – get it?) Anyway, I was in a dilemma when Quill (and how fabulous is that name?) spoke to me again.

'Tell 'er that Freda says she wor a cantankerous old bat when she came ti 'er an' all. And she nivver paid for 'er last readin'.'

OK – dilemma resolved. 'Mrs Proudfoot,' I interrupted. 'I have another message for you.'

Eva stared at me as I relayed the information word for word. The colour drained from her cheeks. 'Who told you that? Who've you been talking to?'

Quill spoke again, so I passed on that message

too. 'My contact also wants me to tell you that the twenty pounds that went missing from your purse yesterday was your son Eddy and that your husband isn't working on the oil rigs in the Middle East, he's living in Bristol with a barmaid called Bridget. And he says that in answer to the question you came here to ask, there's no point in contesting your mother's will and don't even think of selling other people's homes to try and sort out your problems; you'll just have to go out and get a job.'

The curtains fluttered and the temperature rose to that of a pleasant April evening by the fire. I didn't need to look over into the corner to know that Quill had gone.

For several seconds Eva was silent. Then she pulled out a piece of crumpled tissue and dabbed her eyes. 'No one knows that our Percy ran off with Bridget Braithwaite from the Crab and Cockle. Not even our Eddy – he thinks his dad's been in Dubai for the last eighteen months. I don't know how I'm going to manage. Me and Percy bought a little house to let out as an investment, but the tenant's in arrears with the rent. I was counting on Mother's money.' Suddenly, she stiffened, bustled her bosom into the horizontal position and stood up with a murderous expression. 'And as for our Eddy – the thieving little—'

'I feel the spirits drawing away now,' Wanda interjected, frowning at me and shaking her head disapprovingly.

'Spirits drawing away my elbow!' snapped Eva, as she moved towards the door. 'I've seen halibut with more psychic ability than you.' Then she looked at me. 'But that lass of yours – now she's got the gift.'

As Eva Proudfoot slammed the front door, Wanda got up and went upstairs without speaking to me. I could hear her banging and clattering and I knew she was doing what she always does when she's upset, packing up ready to move on. Great! So not only had I got my friends into trouble but now I'd put Wanda's nose out of joint too. If this was a gift, then I didn't want to sound ungrateful, but I'd really rather send it back and exchange it for something useful, like a decent singing voice, or artistic ability – or a kitten.

That was it! I would buy Wanda a kitten. An adorable fluffy little pet would not only cheer her up but it would also make it harder for her to leave. What a stroke of genius!

5

Talk about the Universe moving in mysterious ways! How was I to know that Wanda's friendly trawlerman and landlord, Teddy, was the single father of Kameran's best mate and tennis partner, Kevin Dobson? And, even more amazingly, it turns out that the Dobsons' pedigree Persian cat had recently gone AWOL. They'd found her two days later getting jiggy with a neighbour's common-or-garden moggy, and the resulting three little balls of fluff were just about ready for adoption. So when I phoned Kameran and asked where in Whitby I could find a kitten at eight o'clock on a Monday evening, before you could say Macavity the Mystery Cat, Teddy was round on the doorstep with a cat basket in one hand and a bunch of flowers in the other. What a result! A pet *and* a love-interest in one go. Surely Wanda couldn't do a runner now.

I gave Teddy the once-over and I was quite impressed. In fact, he'd scrubbed up so well that I didn't recognise him at first. I'd only ever seen him in oilskins and a fisherman's gansey, so to see him on the doorstep in fairly presentable jeans and jacket was definitely encouraging. His unruly beard had been tamed and combed and, wait for this – his usually windswept hair was tied back in a ponytail! (Wanda's always been a sucker for a man with a ponytail.)

I wasn't so sure about his attempt to clean up his act on the fragrance front, though. True, it was definitely a good move to get rid of the nasally-challenging aroma of fish and sea salt, but it smelled as though he'd just masked it under several litres of aftershave – sadly not all from the same bottle. He now smelled less like a bag of rancid crisps and more like an explosion in an aromatherapy clinic. Overall, though, on a scale of Shrek to Johnny Depp, he was definitely moving in the right direction. I was hoping that Teddy's new image might scrape him at least a couple of dates – which would give me a bit longer to work on Wanda to stay.

'Wanda!' I called upstairs. 'Teddy's here to see you.'

'Good,' she shouted down. 'I need him to take us across the Channel. I'm thinking Denmark sounds nice. What do you think, sweetie? Copenhagen grab you?'

Hmm! Not quite the response I was hoping for.

'I'll leave you two to it.' I gave Teddy one of my two-eyed winks and grabbed the mobile phone that Wanda and I share. 'Good luck,' I whispered and tiptoed out of the door. If this worked, I was definitely going into the matchmaking business, what with my success this afternoon with Kameran and Milly, and now Teddy turning up looking like a serious contender – I might have just found my new niche in life.

I grabbed the rainbow jacket that Wanda had knitted me for the winter solstice last year and headed towards the town. First I phoned Milly, but her mother answered and said she was grounded because of the whole detention thing. Next I tried Amanpreet, but she was baby-sitting her little brother, so as a last resort I gave Kameran a ring.

'Hi,' he said. 'No, not doing a thing. I've done my homework and I'm just playing PSP. It's Mum's book group night and Dad's on call at the medical centre.' Both Kameran's parents are doctors. He's got an older sister but she's away at university. 'Do you fancy getting some chips?'

'Will there be anywhere open at this time?' I asked.

'Course – the chippy by the harbour.'

I keep forgetting that when people say chips around here, they mean fries. 'Cool, I'll meet you there in five.'

The thing about Whitby is it's *so* hilly. The whole town straddles the river and the houses are built up the cliffs on either bank, so it doesn't matter where you go, you have to have legs like a Himalayan Sherpa. When Kameran suggested meeting at the chip shop I thought my calf muscles could have the night off because the harbour's on one level, but by the time we were halfway through our chips, he'd headed up the steep, meandering path to the West Cliff.

'I feel sorry for Milly, being grounded like that, don't you?' I'd been trying to pump him for some sort of hint about how my first attempt as a lonely hearts counsellor was going.

'Suppose so.' But he just wasn't playing ball. 'Have you been travelling around for long?'

'As long as I can remember, really. She's very pretty, don't you think? And really cool too?'

He looked across at me and frowned. 'Who?'

Durr! Who did he think I was talking about? 'Milly, of course.'

He shrugged. 'Guess so. It must be amazing to have been to as many countries as you have.

Where's the most exciting place you've lived?'

'Anywhere can be exciting if you want it to be.' I was getting the hint – he didn't want to talk about the new love of his life, even though he'd wanted my assistance in the early stages. On the positive side, though, at least it meant he wasn't going to turn into one of those kiss 'n' tell guys.

'No way!' he said. 'How can you say *anywhere* can be interesting? I mean, look at this place: it's so boring it gives boredom a bad name.' We'd finally got to the top of the West Cliff. 'We get a couple of months in the summer when it hots up a bit, but other than that, look at it . . .' Kameran turned and did an expansive gesture with his arms, '. . . it's dead.'

'Oh come on!' I argued. 'There's loads of interesting stuff here.' I pointed across the river to the ruins of the abbey on the cliff top at the other side. 'Whitby's got so much history . . .'

Kameran shrugged and gave a little grin. 'I rest my case – what's history if it's not just a bunch of dead people!'

'Well, you've got Dracula. You can't say Dracula's not interesting.'

'Great – a bunch of *un*-dead people!' He smiled, then stuck two fries under his top lip like a vampire and raised his arms above his head. 'Fangs for everyfing,' he said in a creepy voice.

'Seriously,' I laughed. 'I like it here. I'm trying to persuade Wanda to stay.'

He shook his head and smiled. 'I can't wait to leave. When I've finished school, I'm going to live in New York, or Paris, or . . .' He screwed up his chip paper and threw it at the litter bin, scoring a direct hit. 'Or . . .' But before he could list his top ten places to live, he stopped and his eyes widened to the size of saucers. 'Whoa! Look at that.' He was pointing out to sea.

I peered into the dark of the North Sea and could just make out a wall of grey cloud rolling in towards the land, like a gigantic, ghostly steam-roller.

'Oh my days! What on earth is it?' I gasped.

'A sea fret,' he said, grabbing the sleeve of my jacket and pulling me towards the road.

'A sea what?'

'Fret – it's like a thick mist that comes off the sea,' he explained. 'Come on, we ought to go home. We'll be better going back through the town than along the harbour.'

He jogged my arm and I dropped what was left of my fries on the pavement.

'Hold on,' I said, bending down to pick them up.

'Just leave them,' Kameran chivvied.

'I couldn't possibly!' I was shocked. 'That's not environmentally friendly.'

'Maybe not, but it's seagull friendly, and I want to get you home before the fog gets too thick.'

'And what about the rats?' I asked. 'If everyone just threw down their food and left it, we'd be overrun with rats.'

I gathered up the last of the chips and walked over to the litter bin, but as I turned back towards the road and Kameran, the blanket of thick wet mist swirled across the wide grass verge and enveloped us. I've heard people talk about pea-soupers but this was more like a Hungarian Goulasher – with dumplingser! I couldn't even see Kameran and he'd only been a couple of metres away.

'Where are you?' I reached out and began groping around in front of me. The air was cold and clammy and I could feel droplets of drizzle on my face, but no hint of Kameran.

'It's OK. I'm here,' he said. But his voice seemed distant and it was hard to tell which direction it was coming from.

'Where?' I called, tapping my foot ahead of me to try and feel my way.

'Hereeee . . .' And he trailed off into eerie silence.

'Kameran?' I was starting to get spooked out. 'Wherever you are, just stand still and I'll try to find you.'

I thought if I followed his voice we were bound to meet up, but he didn't answer. I strained my ears but there was no sound. And I mean *no* sound! None at all – except for the sea, of course; there was still some muted lapping at the bottom of the cliff. But, apart from that, silence – no sound of cars crawling through the fog, no boat engines chugging into the harbour, no foghorns, no music – nothing. It was like I was suddenly in a vacuum.

'Kameran!' This wasn't funny any more.

And then I had another realisation – as well as there being no sound, there was no light either. No streetlights filtering through the mist, no fuzzy yellow headlights on the road ahead, no lights from the hotels across the road. What sort of scary fog was this? Surely some light would've diffused through the mist.

I fumbled in my pocket and got out my phone. All I had to do was press the last number I'd dialled and Kameran and I could meet up by speaking to each other – why hadn't I thought of that before? You can tell I'm not used to having a mobile. But there seemed to be yet another problem – the little green light that comes on the screen just wasn't happening. I pressed and pressed but nothing. Brilliant! The battery must have gone. That was so typical of Wanda! She makes sure it's charged during the day when clients want to ring her but when I need it – zilch!

I took a deep breath and began pushing one foot forward, tentatively feeling my way towards the road, so that I didn't fall down the kerb. But the weirdest thing was, the ground under my feet wasn't the smooth, firm stone of the pavement I was expecting; it was soft and spongy. I tapped my toe around, searching for something solid, but all I could feel was lumpy, bumpy earth. Maybe, I thought, I'd accidentally turned round and was back on the grass verge again, so I did a hundred and eighty degree pivot and started edging my way in the other direction. I'm not sure how far I'd gone, it couldn't have been more than half a dozen steps, but there was still no hint of a footpath, road or any other man-made surface – in fact, the grass seemed to be getting tuftier and the ground more uneven.

Suddenly, my foot slipped into a dip and my ankle gave way.

'Owwww!' I cried as I collapsed sideways into the mud and wet, then I let out a frustrated 'Ohhhhh!' and banged the ground with my fist. Wanda's always impressed upon me the necessity of expressing anger rather than letting it build up inside. And believe me, it certainly helped.

So, not being one to dwell on negativity, I manoeuvred myself on to all fours and started groping my way across the grass. The road couldn't be much further; we'd been standing right on the edge and I'd only walked to the litter bin. Yet, as I groped around, I could feel patches of clay and pebbles – but not a hint of a paving stone! And then:

'Tha munt go too far. 'Tis dangerous.'

Oh great! Just what I needed right now – my friendly neighbourhood ghost to pop up.

'Now is really not a good time, Quill,' I said, still crawling on all fours.

'T'cliff'll give way like it did wi' me. Tha munt go no further,' Quill warned.

'I'm not going towards the cliff, I'm trying to find the road,' I said, sounding a bit sharp.

'Baint no road up 'ere.'

'Of course there's a road. It's the one that runs along the West Cliff out to the golf course.'

Wonderful! Other people get spirits who guide them and give them uplifting messages; I get one who thinks he's the after-life's answer to the Ordnance Survey! I was just about to tell him to go away and stop being ridiculous when my hand found something like a thick piece of wood sticking upright. I breathed a sigh of relief. At last, it must be one of the huge whale's jawbones that form an archway at the top of the cliff. As much as I detest the thought of the poor dead whale giving up its mouth parts just for decoration, I was very grateful to it at that moment. At least I knew where I was.

'Ah'm not daft, tha knows,' Quill said.

'I didn't say you were.' I used the jawbone to pull myself up to my feet again.

'No, but tha thowt it,' he said in an accusatory tone.

OK, I'd been found out and I wasn't proud of it. 'I'm sorry,' I said. 'I was feeling a little anxious because I didn't know where I was, but now I've found the whale's jawbones, I'll be fine. I can find my way from here.'

'Baint no whale's jawbones.'

I was becoming exasperated. 'Look, Quill, I just want to go home, all right? I've found a landmark that I recognise, so I'll just be on my way. Thank you for coming to visit me – again!' I added a bit tersely. 'But really – I'll be fine.'

' 'Tis t'signal flag,' he said, flatly.

'What do you mean it's the signal flag? What signal flag?'

'T'beacon. There's one on t'East Cliff an' all. Ti warn of enemy ships coming across t'German Ocean.'

I felt up the shaft of the thing in my hand, and sure enough it felt less like bone and more like wood. And there were notches on it as though twigs had been cut off. I stretched out my hand and felt another to the left. Taking hold of that one, I moved round until I'd counted six long wooden poles in a circle, each one bending inwards slightly so that I didn't need to be a mathematician to realise that they probably converged somewhere way over my head. I know I'd only been in Whitby a couple of weeks, but how come I'd never seen this signal flag? I'd been up on the West Cliff a few times, not to mention being able to see it from my bedroom window.

Something weird was going on and I wasn't sure what it was but it was creeping me out. Despite the freezing cold, I was starting to sweat.

'Kameran!' I called out again. 'Where are

you?' I was in serious need of some company –
living company.

And then, as quickly as it had appeared, the fog
lifted. I could hear the lapping of the waves quite
clearly now and the gulls were circling overhead
again. Phew! Panic over. For a moment there I'd
started to freak out. Now all I wanted to do was
find Kameran and go home.

The moon was bright and full, casting a white
light across the field – hold on, the field? Just how
far had I walked in the fog? I looked across the
estuary to the opposite cliff and saw the ruins of
the abbey and the church, just as they had been
earlier. But right where I was standing everything
had changed. For a start, there was the tall wooden
structure Quill had told me was the signal flag –
that hadn't been there before. But more alarmingly,
the huge Victorian building of the County Hotel on
the corner had completely disappeared, as had all
the other hotels and houses. And, just as Quill had
said, there were no whale's jawbones – and no
statue of Captain Cook, and no road.

But more worrying than any of that – there was
no Kameran!

6

I came to the decision that either I must have fallen into a coma and sleepwalked several miles along the coast to some deserted spot that looked scarily similar to Whitby – or Wanda had been putting funny honey in my camomile tea again.

In the absence of anyone who was actually breathing to come to my assistance, I turned to Quill for an explanation. 'What's going on?'

'Ah need ti show thi summat,' he said, walking, or rather drifting in the direction of the town.

'Whoa! Hold on there, Spirit Boy,' I replied. 'I'm not going anywhere till I find out where I am and where my friend's gone.'

He turned and gave me this intense but, ohmylord, totally yummy look. 'Ah'm tekkin' thi ti see summat important. Tha's got ti trust mi.'

I put my hands on my hips and stood my ground. 'OK, two things – first, you *still* haven't answered my question. And second, you're going to have to start speaking in a way that I don't have to translate every single word. Surely, if you've been hanging around for a quarter of a millennium, you must have picked up some of the lingo?'

He cocked his head on one side and raised an eyebrow. 'Tha's bin travelling t'world all thi life, but duss tha speak owt but t'King's English?'

Don't you just hate a clever clogs? 'I think you'll find it's the *Queen's* English at the moment,' I corrected. 'Anyway, it shows what you know; I can say "Hello" in eleven languages – twelve if you include "G'day" in Australian.'

We stood there, eyeballing each other – well, I stood and Quill floated. Neither of us was willing to make the first move. Quill folded his arms as though he'd got all the time in the world – which, when you think about it, he had. So in the end it was down to me.

'OK, I'll come with you but only on condition that you tell me what's happened to my friend,' I told him. 'I mean, excuse me for sounding paranoid, but one minute I'm enjoying a pleasant evening stroll and the next it's as though I've slipped through a time warp into a parallel—' And then it dawned on me. 'Holy Karoly! That's what happened, isn't it? I've gone into a parallel universe.'

Quill shrugged. ' 'Tis more a goin' back through

t'ages. Look 'ee ovver yonder.'

He was pointing inland, a little away from the town towards the silhouette of a windmill. But I was too busy trying to get my head round his last statement to take in what he was showing me. He'd said it so casually, like most people would say, 'Oh, I'm just popping to the shops.' Only this time it was, 'Oh, I've just popped back a few hundred years.' I know that I've been reincarnated masses of times – but genuine time travel? This was mind-blowing. I couldn't wait to tell Wanda! Although, on second thoughts, I'd have to wait and see if she'd forgiven me for the Eva Proudfoot episode. I didn't want her getting jealous again – it really wasn't good for her karma.

'So does that mean that if I hang around for a couple of hundred years, Kameran'll be right here groping around in the fog?' I asked.

Quill nodded distractedly; his eyes were still fixed on a spot in the distance. 'Aye.'

And then a thought occurred to me. 'I won't *have* to wait that long, though, will I? I mean, I will be able to go back and see Wanda and my friends again – soon?' I was trying to keep the panic out of my voice. I like to think of my reincarnations as generally being of a spiritual progression kind of thing; going backwards definitely doesn't feature on any of the paths to Nirvana that I've come across.

'Daint fret thissen. There be more important things afoot.'

'OK,' I said, with more than a hint of irritation in my voice. 'Enough of all the thees and thous and yees and yays and thissens and wissens. You are going to have to talk at least *half* twenty-first century if you don't want me to go into total brain overload.'

'Ah'm sorry. I'll try,' he conceded. 'It was never my intent to upset thi . . . thee . . . you.' He paused then looked at me with a puzzled expression. 'What's a wissen?'

I flapped my hand. 'Who knows? It has a nice ring to it, though. Now, what is it you want to show me, because as exciting as this time travel stuff is, I'd like to get home; I have college in the morning.'

'Come.'

He beckoned me to follow him, and before I knew what was happening, we were about a quarter of a mile inland standing on a rough path near the windmill that a couple of minutes ago had been in the distance. Wow! This zooming about was fun.

In front of us was a group that looked as though it was on its way to a Hallowe'en party. There were three people draped in white sheets like ghosts, leading a couple of donkeys. The donkeys had their hooves wrapped in sacks to muffle the sound and, although they were fully laden, they were also draped in fabric except for their heads.

When they reached the mill, the men pulled off their sheets – and I almost freaked out because there in front of us was another Quill!

'Oh my days – there are two of you?' I looked to my Quill for an explanation. 'Do you have an evil twin, or am I starting to see double with all this going back through time thing?'

' 'Tis me when I was alive,' Quill whispered, then nodded in the direction of the group, indicating that I should watch them.

'This is probably a stupid question, but why were you dressed up as a ghost?' I asked. 'Have you never heard of tempting fate?'

He was still staring at the scene in front of us. ' 'Twas to scare off prying eyes. If folk thought there was a ghost on t'road, they'd be not inclined to venture forth.'

'Still, nice touch of irony, don't you think?'

He gave me a look that would have curdled

custard. ' 'Twas how the contrabandiers distributed their cargoes free from fear of being seen. Word was put about that a haunting was due and folk closed t'shutters and stayed indoors.'

What was I hearing? 'Wow! You were a smuggler? How exciting!'

'There's nowt exciting about it. 'Twere dangerous and difficult work but it gave a few extra bob to families that needed it and put a drop of good rum on tables that wouldn't otherwise afford it. Now, sssh!'

I gave him a querying look. 'OK, so if you cast your mind back ... ooo, let's say, a couple of hundred years or so ... to when you were standing there with your mates, are you seriously telling me you could hear someone whispering?'

'No.'

Aha! Got him! 'So why are you telling me to be quiet?'

' 'Tis not so they won't hear, 'tis so that *you'll* listen.' Humph! Get him! It felt like I'd just been told off by a teacher. 'My mam allus says, you can't hear if your mouth's oppen,' he went on, pointing in the direction of the men.

Cheek! I was just about to argue – but then I realised that he probably had a point. So I closed my mouth and edged forward along the road, all the time watching the little group who were standing uncertainly in front of the mill. The living Quill wiped the back of his hand across his brow.

'Isaac, be off wi' thi,' he said to one of the older men. 'Me an' Robert can 'andle it from 'ere. Tha's got a bairn on t'way. Get thissen 'ome ti 'Lizabeth. Dusty Miller'll be out presently.'

Oh great! I'd just got the ghostly Quill to talk in a way that I could at least partly understand and now I was having to translate this lot. Why couldn't I have been visited by a more contemporary spirit?

My Quill leaned forward and whispered to me, 'That's Isaac Chapman. We worked in Coates's shipyard as carpenters. I'd been serving my apprenticeship this two year, but Isaac was a journeyman. T'other lad was Isaac's brother-in-law, Robert Elstob. Poor old Robert – if you put 'is brains in a bee, it'd fly backwards.'

I giggled. Not only was he gorgeous, he was funny too! Just my luck to have been born two hundred and fifty years too late!

'Isaac Chapman?' I queried. 'He's not an ancestor of Kameran's friend Joel Chapman, by any chance?' I thought of joking Joel who'd come to me for a reading.

Quill nodded. 'Aye – family's lived in Whitby since time. That's who I need you to help. But just watch what happens.'

I turned back and watched the scene unfold in front of the windmill.

'Nay, lad,' Isaac said. 'Tha'll need all t'elp tha can get wi' young barley-brain 'ere.' He ruffled Robert's hair. 'Fancy turning up wi' daft beasts like yon! Ah said ti fetch ponies, not donkeys, tha daft lummox!'

The living Quill was looking round outside the mill. 'Leave 'im be, Isaac. 'Appen 'e's only ten pence ti t'shillin' but 'e means no 'arm and 'e's a good worker.'

'Ten pence ti t'guinea, more like.' Isaac smiled and gave his brother-in-law an affectionate shove. 'When Ah wed thi sister, Ah nivver thowt Ah'd be weddin' thee an all.'

Quill was scrabbling around on the ground by the mill, obviously looking for something. 'Ah can't see t'sacks that Dusty said 'e'd leave out.'

Then Robert took something out of his pocket and began striking it like a match.

Immediately, Isaac snatched it away. 'By 'eck,

lad! What's tha think tha's doin' lightin' a tinderbox? It baint enough that t'fog's lifted, leaving us on show for all ti see, tha wants ti give t'Riding Officer a light ti guide 'im reet ti us an' all!'

To be honest, I could've done with Robert's tinderbox throwing a bit of light on the scene – it was difficult to make out what was happening. There was a lot of whispering and dithering and looking round the mill, but there didn't appear to be much action.

'What's going on?' I asked Quill's ghost. 'Am I missing something?'

'We were supposed to deliver t'goods to t'Union Mill and leave it in sacks for the miller to conceal in a consignment of flour. But when we got there, there were no sacks. Look what happens next.'

The living Quill stopped suddenly and beckoned for the others to move away from the mill towards the road.

'Ah smell a rat,' he whispered.

'Aye,' Robert said slowly. ' 'Twill be t'wheat as attracts 'em.'

'Nay,' Quill said, patiently, 'Ah daint mean a *real* rat – Ah mean summat's afoot. Baint like Dusty ti let folk down.'

The three of them looked around anxiously. Then Isaac spoke.

'Let's leave it any'ow. 'E's likely still down at t'inn. 'E can tek it in when 'e gets 'ome.'

The living Quill shook his head. 'Ah'm uneasy aboot it. Summat's not reet. Ah reckon t'Preventive men 'ave got wind. Isaac, go 'ome. Ah knows 'Lizabeth's confinement's overdue. Me an' Robert'll tek this lot down ti t'Old Mulgrave Castle and stash it there.'

'Nay,' Isaac said. ' 'Tis three set out this neet, and 'tis three will go 'ome. Come, let's away.'

The ghostly Quill shook his head sadly. 'Oh Isaac, if only tha'd listened to me.' Then he turned to me. 'Come on,' he said, indicating for me to follow him.

'*Now* where are we go—?' But before the words had left my lips, we were back at the top of the cliff, although further along from where we'd started out. The moonlight revealed a tumbledown cottage built on the grassy slope which, about fifty metres ahead, crumbled down into the sea. There was a rough wooden fence around the cottage and a narrow path running a few metres in front of it.

'T'Old Mulgrave Castle,' my Quill said.

'It doesn't look much like a castle to me,' I

commented, seeing the ramshackle collection of buildings and outbuildings.

' 'Tis an inn. It fell into t'sea a hundred year afore you were born. But in my day, 'twas a hive of activity for contrabandiers and was where t'landers used to store goods that they unloaded from boats.' Quill pointed down to the beach below. 'There's caves down there full of the finest wines and spirits to grace any table.'

'Wow!' I was intrigued. And Kameran said history wasn't interesting! He should've come with me – then he'd see how interesting it is. But something a bit less romantic than smugglers and their contraband was a heavy, choking smell in the air. I started coughing. 'Ugh! What on earth is that disgusting smell?'

'T'limekiln yonder.' Quill pointed a little way behind the inn to where there was a huddle of cottages and the glowing fires of a kiln.

'Boy, did they need to learn about aromas and the effect they have on the body!' I wafted my hand over my nose. 'What's it for?'

'T'farmers spread it on their land to improve t'yield,' he replied distractedly. Then he shook his head sadly. 'We never intended to come to Upgang tonight,' he said, gazing back along the road towards the mill. 'In t'morning, Isaac and me had had word that Jenny was coming – that was t'code for a delivery of cargo from t'continent. A sloop was coming into dock. They pretended it was for repair.' He gave an ironic smile. 'But what they meant was we had to go on board and take t'contraband out of t'false keel. It wasn't a big run; just a few half-ankers of brandy, a couple of bags of tea, a roll of French velvet and some tobacco. There was a lugger due into Upgang that night from Flushing in t'Low Countries. It had a huge cargo of gin, Aarrach and drugges . . .'

'Drugs!' I was shocked. 'Are you trying to tell me you were a drug smuggler? Well, I'm sorry but—'

'Nay!' Quill shook his head. 'Drugges, as in camphor, cardamom and julep.'

'Oh, well, if you mean spices, you should say spices. I mean, you say drugs and you think . . . never mind what you think.'

Quill was shaking his head, but this time in despair. 'Most of t'men were going to be landing t'lugger's cargo, so me and Isaac reckoned we could manage. Of course Robert overheard us and wanted a part so Isaac set him to fetch three ponies from Tom Sutcliffe's farm. We'd done it afore; we'd borrow them for a run, then, when we took them back, we'd leave a keg of brandy in t'stable for Tom's trouble and a yard of finest French lace for t'mistress.'

'Only Robert didn't get the ponies, he got a couple of donkeys,' I said, just to show him that I had been paying attention.

'Aye, that was an ill omen to start with. Not exactly t'fleetest of beasts. Just when you need a bit of speed, they're as likely to put their heads down and dig their heels in.' He sighed heavily. 'Then t'fog lifted, which no one had accounted for. But what we didn't know . . .' He looked down the road towards the mill and saw the shapes of himself, Isaac and Robert heading towards the inn. 'Hey up. Watch careful now.'

The three men arrived at the inn and walked their donkeys round to the front of the building. Isaac handed the reins to Quill while he began unfastening the small barrels from the first donkey.

Robert went round the back of the second donkey and began unfastening the barrels as his brother-in-law was doing.

'Nay, leave it, lad,' Isaac warned.

But he was too late. The small, squat tubs that had been suspended over the donkey's back suddenly crashed to the ground and rolled away towards the edge of the cliff. But worse, they startled the donkeys. The two animals began bucking and kicking, and one caught Robert in a very sensitive place with its hoof. He collapsed on to the ground groaning and wailing.

It was a scene of absolute chaos: donkeys braying, Robert crying, Isaac shouting at Robert to stop his howling before every preventive officer on the east coast was alerted, and Quill running and tumbling in the dark to try and catch the brandy before it rolled over the edge of the cliff and was smashed on the sands at the bottom.

'Oh my days! What a nightmare! Did you lose the brandy?' I asked my Quill.

He gave an ironic smile. 'Would that were all I lost that night.'

Suddenly, from the direction of the limekiln, I heard a noise. I looked up and saw the silhouettes of perhaps twenty men riding towards us on horseback. The moonlight flashed as they advanced and I couldn't quite make out what was happening. Were they the other smugglers who'd been waiting for the lugger from Holland to land on the beach below? Then, with a terrible realisation, I saw that the men were dressed in scarlet coats, white breeches and three-cornered hats. They were soldiers! And the flashes had been the moonlight reflected on their swords.

One of the soldiers dismounted, grabbed Robert by the shoulder, hauled him to his feet and held a pistol to his head.

'Oh no!' I gasped. 'They're not going to kill Robert, are they? I can't stand death – well, not other people's anyway.'

I could hardly bear to watch, so I put my hands over my eyes and just peeped out between my fingers. This was awful! Another man, this one in a blue uniform, rode up to the soldier at the front.

'Josiah Proudfoot!' my Quill almost spat. 'T'Riding Officer – traitor!'

Well, that figures!

Josiah Proudfoot pointed to where Isaac had joined Quill, both of them still running to catch the barrels. 'Shoot! Shoot! They be getting away.'

The soldier at the front raised a long musket to his shoulder and pointed it straight at the living Quill. 'Yield at the King's command or die!'

Uh oh!

7

'Come with me,' spirit Quill said, and suddenly we were standing by the edge of the cliff where the other Quill and Isaac were crouched down on the grassy slope.

Isaac rolled to one side and pulled something from the waistband of his breeches. I screwed up my eyes to try and see what it was and was shocked to realise that it was a long, wooden-handled pistol.

'Oh no!' I turned away from the scene. 'I'm sorry, but there's no way I can condone the use of firearms,' I said to my Quill. 'I'm afraid the two of you have lost my sympathy vote now. Take me back to my own time, please.'

He tutted. 'By – you might be a comely maid, but you're an impatient one. Just watch, will you?'

Ooo! Comely? I wasn't sure what it meant but, from the tone of his voice, I was pretty sure he'd just been flirting with me. I felt my cheeks burning and gave him a little smile. 'OK, fire away ...' Then, remembering the circumstances, I checked myself. 'I didn't mean that literally!'

But it was too late! There was a flash of fire and the crack of a gun, but not from Isaac – it came from the direction of the inn where the soldiers were holding Robert. I couldn't bear to look.

'Did they shoot Robert?' I asked faintly.

'Nay. They weren't shooting at Robert,' he replied. 'They were shooting at me.'

'What?' I could hardly believe my ears. 'You're not trying to tell me that you've brought me here to witness your death, are you? Because that wouldn't just be morbid, it would be totally inappropriate.'

Before he could answer, I heard the living Quill whisper, 'Put tha pistol away, Isaac. 'Twill only aggravate t'matter. T'penalty for being caught wi that lot baint more than a fine. But if tha pulls a pistol on t'King's men, we'll both be dancing in t'air at York Castle afore t'year's out.'

I turned to my Quill for a translation. 'Dancing in the air? Was the penalty to get conscripted into some sort of aerial formation dance team?' I was trying to visualise an eighteenth-century Riverdance in midair, but couldn't quite get my head round it.

He gave me another look that would've soured

honey. 'It means hanging,' he said coldly.

I gasped. So that was what all the stuff about the Hanged Man tarot card was about when Quill visited me in the PE cupboard. He was trying to tell me that he'd been hanged. Oh no! This was too awful for words. 'I really would like to go home now, please,' I said as politely as I could. 'I've seen all I want to, thank you.'

'What we want isn't allus what we need,' my Quill said, never taking his eyes off the two men lying face-down in the grass on the cliff top. 'You'll see.'

The living Quill was pleading with Isaac. ' 'Tis better to pay a fine, Isaac, please.'

'Aye, that's as mebbe, but Ah baint got 'undred pound ti mi name,' Isaac replied, looking round as though he was doing a recce for an escape route. 'And Ah'm sure as 'eck not made up wi t'idea of being impressed in ti t'navy for five year while 'Lizabeth and t'bairn end up in t'poorhouse. Nay, Quill lad, Ah'm tekkin mi chances.'

Isaac began to slither down the grassy slope towards the edge of the cliff when Robert's voice rang out.

'Isaac, help us! 'E says 'e's going ti blow mi brains out! Isaac! Quill! Come back.'

I heard Isaac groan, then say under his breath, 'Tha 'as ti 'ave brains afore they can blow 'em out, tha daft beggar.'

The living Quill stood up. 'Come on, Isaac. They know us names. We'd best give ussens up. Tha'll be no use as a faither if tha's at t'end of t'angman's noose.'

Isaac threw down the pistol with a sense of resignation. ' 'Twere only ti scare 'em any'ow. Ah'd neither powder nor shot.' He shook his head. 'Ah'll bet it's oor Robert what's give us away. That sly owd fox Proudfoot'd go ti any ends ti get information, even plyin' a poor doit like Robert wi' ower much ale.'

We watched the two of them begin to walk back towards Josiah Proudfoot and the dragoons, but they'd taken no more than a couple of steps when there was a terrible rumbling underfoot and cracks started appearing in the earth where we were standing.

'What's going on?' I asked my Quill. 'It feels like a mini earthquake.'

'Aye,' he replied. 'An earth-tremor was felt through all of t'North Riding that night. 'Twas just our luck, eh? No ponies, no fog, betrayed by t'Riding Officer and then an earth-tremor. Was ever a venture more ill-fated?'

Now when Wanda and I were in Mexico, the kids there said that an earthquake is when El Diablo – that's the devil in Spanish (you see, I *can* speak more than one language) – rips up the ground from the inside so that he and his friends can come out and make trouble on earth. In terms of the earthquakes that I've experienced, this one was fairly feeble, but if this was El Diablo's way of making trouble for Quill and his mates, then he was doing a pretty good job. The donkeys began bucking and braying again, the soldiers' horses started rearing up and whinnying and everyone, including Quill and Isaac, started to freak out big-time.

'Run!' Isaac shouted to the living Quill. 'T'cliff's goin'!'

'Stop!' screamed one of the soldiers. 'You are our prisoners. In the name of the King, stand still.'

Yeah, right! Like anyone could stand still when the ground beneath their feet was wobbling like a giant jelly.

'We are done for,' Isaac called to the living Quill as he threw himself forwards to land face-down on the trembling grass.

Quill made to follow his friend but, as the

tremor subsided, a fissure opened up in front of him.

'Jump lad!' yelled Isaac.

'Jump!' I screamed.

I watched in horror as the living Quill tried to leap forward, but as his back foot pushed off, tons of earth and grass began crumbling away, forcing him to lose his footing. He stumbled forward, desperately grabbing for anything to save himself.

'Do something!' I screamed at the spirit Quill as we stood helplessly watching the cliff face slide down on to the beach.

He shrugged. 'History is history. Cannot be altered.'

'So why have you brought me here? Take me back, I'm not watching any more!'

'Wait,' he said, never taking his eyes off his living self.

Did I say earlier that he was gorgeous? Well, strike that; he's nothing more than a malicious sadist – making me witness horrible things like this.

The living Quill reached up and grabbed a tussock of grass and I breathed a sigh of relief.

'Phew!' I said. 'I thought for a minute there you were going to make me watch you fall over the cliff.'

My Quill said nothing – which, I must confess, made me a little bit twitchy.

I watched Isaac pull himself on his stomach back to where Quill was clutching the tuft of turf.

'Quick – give us thi 'and,' he whispered urgently, reaching out to his friend.

Quill stretched out the fingers of his right hand towards Isaac. I was holding my breath, willing them to make contact. The tips of Quill's fingers touched Isaac's and Isaac nudged forward, trying to get a tighter grip. All this tension was doing my nerves no good at all. I saw Quill give an almighty lurch and lock his fingers over Isaac's and I started to relax a little. Uh oh – too soon; the voice of Josiah Proudfoot, the Riding Officer, rang out.

'They're escaping! Shoot them!'

There was another flash and a second shot cracked through the air. A dull *phut* sounded as the bullet hit the clump of grass next to Quill's hand – or at least, I thought it had hit the clump of grass next to Quill's hand.

'Ow!' he yelped. In the moonlight I could just make out the pale fingers of his left hand. 'Isaac,' he cried out. 'Ah can't hold on.' And then, 'Aaaaagggghh!'

'Nooooooo!' I yelled.

'Are you all right, love?' An old woman with a Yorkshire terrier was standing next to me. The dog had a pale blue bow in its hair and the woman was carrying a yellow plastic pooper-scooper. Now, I'm no historian, but I'm pretty sure that no one pooper-scooped in Quill's day.

I looked round me. There was a light mist and it was quite dark where I was standing, but I was pleased to see that there were streetlights glowing their fuzzy yellow glow, and buildings too, and cars crawling along the road.

'I'm fine, thank you,' I said, with more than a hint of relief at being back in the twenty-first century.

Suddenly there was a jingly-jangly rendition of the Bob Dylan song 'Like a Rolling Stone' coming from the pocket of my rainbow jacket. I have asked Wanda to choose a ringtone that isn't prehistoric, but she says it's symbolic. Right at that moment, though, I didn't care. I was just glad to be back and with a phone that seemed to be working. I took it out of my pocket and saw Kameran's number flashing up.

The old lady started to walk away. 'Come on, Brutus,' she said to the tiny dog, then tutted. 'Young folks nowadays!'

'Where are you?' Kameran asked.

I did a quick geographical survey and decided I was about half a mile from where I'd last seen him.

'If you walk along the promenade,' I told him, 'I'll walk towards you. I'll see you in about ten minutes.'

'Ten minutes!' he exclaimed. 'How the heck did you manage to wander that far?'

'Trust me,' I replied, 'if I told you, you'd never believe me.'

Like I said, I always believe that the truth is the best answer, but sometimes a lie would be so much easier.

8

Fortunately, when I got home, Wanda was so wrapped up in her new pet that I don't think she'd have noticed if I'd staggered in and told her I'd been abducted by aliens. Which was fine by me; the last thing I wanted was to start explaining about my recent foray into time travel in front of Teddy.

'Look, sweetie!' Wanda called from the kitchen. 'I want to introduce you to someone.' I went through and she was holding up this tiny grey fluffy kitten and talking in a voice that was so high-pitched, I'm surprised her crystal ball hadn't shattered. 'Who's a beautiful little kitty, then? Yes you are. Yes you are. You're gorgeous.'

Teddy was sitting in the rocking-chair by the range, looking as though he only needed a pipe and slippers and he'd have been set up until retirement. Talk about too much time travel – it was as though I'd come back half a century early and landed in the cosy domesticity of the nineteen fifties.

'Hi,' I said, mentally debating whether I should

congratulate him for surviving the entire evening with Wanda, or warn him to get his feet out from under the table on a first date. Normally, Wanda's off the starting block like an Olympic athlete if she thinks things are moving too fast. (OK, when I say an Olympic athlete, that's probably not the best analogy, as the only Olympic events that would remotely interest Wanda would be the hundred metres macramé or the freestyle Feng Shui – but I'm sure you get my drift.)

When it comes to men, I don't think Wanda has ever got over my dad. She met him while she was touring the States on a Greyhound bus. When the coach pulled into the bus depot in Kansas City, she tripped over her hippy skirt and fell straight into the arms of Gordon Goodfox, a shaman of the Pawnee Nation. Apparently it was the longest toilet stop in history; nine months and one week to be exact. Then she slung me in a papoose on her back and moved on.

And she's been moving on ever since – especially if someone starts to get too close. So in the interests of my future in Whitby, the last thing I wanted was Teddy thinking he was on to a sure thing. Pleased as I was that my matchmaking had been a success, I needed to cool things down a bit.

Wanda held the kitten up towards me. 'I've called her Mushka,' she cooed.

'Brilliant idea,' I said. Mushka was the name of this little old lady who lived in the apartment next to us in St Petersburg. Her hair was practically the same colour as the kitten's. I took the kitten from Wanda and allowed her to nuzzle into the palm of my hand. Teddy had scored full marks on the kitten front as well as the whole ponytail/casual image thing. In fact, I only needed to sort out some manly fragrances for him and, who knows, he could be Wanda's Mr Right. But if he was going to be in there for the long haul, I really needed to persuade him to play a little hard to get.

'Well, goodnight then, Teddy,' I smiled.

'You off to bed, sweetie?' Wanda asked, taking Mushka from me.

Which was not what I'd intended at all. 'Oh, I thought Teddy was leaving,' I said in my most disingenuous voice, hoping he might take the hint.

Teddy looked startled and made to stand up. 'Er . . . right, then. I'll be off. Thanks for the nettle tea, Wanda. It was just the ticket.'

'No need to go,' Wanda offered. 'Stay and have another cup. It'll do wonders for that touch of rheumatism in your knee. I'll give you some Reiki afterwards too, if you like.'

Teddy sat down again like a shot. 'By, that would be grand.'

I was getting that sinking feeling – this was way too much, way too soon. I really needed to talk to him about the whole Zen philosophy of less is more. But right at that point, I wasn't going to argue. I was totally whacked, so I obliged Wanda and went up to bed.

The following morning I was late for college again, but as soon Milly and Amanpreet saw me in the corridor, they were on to me like an inquisition.

'Come on, then, tell us what happened.'

'Where did you go?'

'What did you do?'

'Whoa!' I put my hands up and adopted the *back off* pose. 'This is worse than when Wanda and I got arrested in Tibet.'

Milly dropped the interrogation and her mouth fell open. 'You've been arrested?'

I shrugged. 'A few times. But Tibet was the worst. I mean, how were we supposed to know that busking wasn't allowed by the occupying Chinese militia?'

'Well . . .' Amanpreet began.

But I cut her off. 'It was a retirical question.'

They were both looking at me in this weird way like I'd got spinach stuck in my teeth.

'You mean *rhetorical*?' Milly asked.

'Whatever.' I flapped my hand. 'But, you know, we had to earn a crust somehow,' I explained, to try and stop them looking at me as though I was one of the Great Train Robbers. 'It wasn't like Wanda could pop into the local Lhasa Job Centre or anything. Although I did tell her I thought "Love Will Set You Free" wasn't the most diplomatic song in her repertoire.'

'Maybe that's why they arrested you,' Milly suggested. 'But still, being a political prisoner is cool.'

Amanpreet looked positively awestruck. 'Wow! What was it like?'

I cleared my throat. 'It sort of went . . . *Loooove will set—*'

'No, not the song!' she interrupted. 'Being arrested; did they torture you?'

'Neh! Just deported us. But put it this way – if you two had had an anglepoise lamp and a pair of handcuffs, you could easily find work in the Drapchi Prison.'

'Oh, ha ha,' Milly grinned. 'Come on, seriously, tell us what happened last night.'

I went as cold as a polar bear in the Arctic! How could they possibly have found out about last night?

'What do you mean?' I asked, sheepishly rummaging in my bag to avoid looking at them.

'With you and Kameran,' Milly persisted.

'Oh that!' Phew – I thought they'd somehow found out about the whole ghost/smuggling/time travel thing. 'How'd you know about that?'

'I saw Kevin Dobson at the bus stop this morning and he told me that you and Kameran had gone out last night.'

Oh dear Lord! There are tribes in the Amazon rainforest whose jungle telegraph is less efficient than this lot. But worse still, just when I was starting to make some headway on the Milly and Kameran love front, she'd got the totally wrong idea and seemed to think that I'd been on some sort of date with him. This was awful.

'Nothing happened,' I said – probably a bit too quickly to sound convincing. 'We just went for a walk and had a bag of chips.'

'Yeah right!' laughed Amanpreet.

But just as I was denying that there was

anything going on between me and Kameran, the voice of Mr Spiggins, the head of year, screeched along the corridor. Mr Spiggins is a small, scrawny man with a toupee that looks about as natural as if he'd got Basil Brush glued to his head. I'm in his group for Geography and he has serious self-esteem issues. He's one of those teachers who would pretend not to notice two bullies punching each other's lights out but then give the most innocuous person in the class a detention for breathing too loudly.

'Kameran Dhillon! Don't run.'

See what I mean? Almost everyone else was pushing and shoving their way along the Technology block corridor, but he picks on Kameran.

'Sorry, sir,' I heard Kameran shout back. The next thing I knew, Kameran had grabbed my arm and, without even acknowledging Milly and Amanpreet, pulled me over to one side of the corridor.

'Listen,' he said urgently, 'can you read palms or anything that doesn't need your cards?'

'Of course,' I replied, trying not to sound too peed off that he had to ask.

'Brilliant! Meet me behind the sports hall at lunch time. I've got some more clients for you.

Got to go, we're late for Technology.' And he shot off.

'Still say nothing's going on?' Amanpreet giggled as she and Milly headed off towards the Resistant Materials room. 'See you at break!'

Oh dear, things were not going at all as I'd planned on the romantic liaison front. At home, I'd got Teddy going way too fast and at school, I'd got Kameran playing way too hard to get. This was going to require some pretty skilful handling.

I was wandering along the corridor towards the Food Technology room, contemplating how I was going to convince Teddy to back off while persuading Kameran to dial it up a bit with Milly, when I heard a stifled shout. There was no one else about so I stopped and listened. Suddenly Joel Chapman, Kameran's friend who'd come to me for a reading the previous day, almost fell out of the boys' toilets and landed on his knees right in front of me.

'Hi, Joel. You OK?' I asked.

But before he could answer, the door opened again and a backpack was lobbed out after him, spilling books and pens all across the floor.

I bent down and picked up a notebook for him.

'It's OK. Just leave it.' He looked flustered.

'Thanks,' he added as an afterthought.

Then the toilet door opened and a large boy with horribly familiar piggy eyes came out. He kicked the backpack and sent it spinning along the corridor.

'Pack it in, Eddy,' Joel said, standing up and eyeing the other boy in the chest. 'I've said I'll get it sorted.'

Now I might have been putting two and two together and coming up with a number in double figures, but I was fairly sure this must be Eddy Proudfoot, the boy who two-timed Milly and stole twenty pounds from his mother's purse.

'You'd better!' Eddy threatened.

I stepped forward. 'Look, I don't know what's going on here, but I'm sure it can be sorted out in a non-confrontational way.'

'Oh look! If it isn't the Freak Fairy!' Eddy sneered. 'Rack off, weirdo! Don't you think you've done enough damage round here already? You and that psycho mother of yours.'

Whoa! Look who's talking when it comes to the *psycho mother* bit, I wanted to say. But I didn't. Eva Proudfoot was one of Wanda's clients and it wouldn't look good to start slagging her off – especially to her own son.

'Come on, Joel.' I picked up some more of Joel's things and pulled him towards the Food Technology room.

'That's right, get a girl to fight your battles for you.' Talk about sexist! I was liking Eddy Proudfoot less and less. 'I'm warning you, Chapman, you've got one week,' he yelled after us.

'Quaking in my wellies!' Joel said casually as he and I headed down the corridor away from Eddy.

'What was all that about?' I asked.

'He wants me to teach him Kung Fu,' Joel laughed, slashing the air and making weird *ha-so* type noises. He looked and sounded less like a martial artist and more like a stick insect with an adenoid problem, but I didn't want to disillusion him. 'I told him; Eddy, my son, no amount of provocation will persuade me to divulge the secrets of the ancients.' Joel tapped the side of his nose knowingly, then made a massive sweep of the air with his arms and kicked open the door to the Food Technology room with the side of his foot.

Unfortunately, Ms Oliver was standing right behind it and she was propelled sideways into one of the cookers. Uh oh! This was my first introduction to Food Technology and I couldn't help thinking it could have gone a lot better.

Ms Oliver stood up, rubbing her elbow, and glared at us. 'Good afternoon,' she said, purposefully looking at her watch. 'Kind of you two to drop in. You can spare me your pathetic excuses for the moment – you can write them down for me over break, which, by the way, you'll be spending with me,' she went on. 'Now, we're working in twos today, so it looks like the pair of you have both drawn short straws – you're together.'

Ms Oliver thrust a sheet of paper at us, which said that we were supposed to be thinking up ideas for a range of luxury fast foods for busy people who enjoy entertaining but don't have much time. Which, actually, I thought sounded pretty cool. I love cooking and if I'd known it was going to be this much fun, I'd have got here earlier.

'OK, I make a mean butternut squash and sunflower seed risotto,' I said to Joel, excitedly. 'We could have that for one of the main course meals. And you should taste my pecan pie. That could be one of the desserts.'

'Oh, sorry,' Joel said cheekily. 'I thought the brief said *luxury*.' He held the paper up to my face and ran his finger along the word. 'Oh yes, so it does. That rules out your ideas – unless we're planning a range of foods for busy *rabbits*!'

'Very funny!' I must admit, although I hardly know Joel, I've always wondered why Kameran is friends with him. He always strikes me as a bit of a lightweight. You know the sort – can't take anything seriously and is always fooling about.

'I suppose you'd rather plan some ready meals for a Neanderthal? Let's see, we could have kebab soup for the starter and some roast kebab for the main course, with kebab sorbet for pudding.'

Joel looked at me and then screwed up the paper. 'Actually,' he said, 'I was thinking more along the lines of using local produce so it would be a seafood-based range. My dad used to have his own seafood restaurant in the Old Town and I want to go to chef school when I leave here and do the same.'

Wow! Now I felt really guilty for thinking badly of him. You see – this is why I should never judge people. You never know what's going on in a person's life. And the more I talked to Joel, the more I realised that there was so much to take seriously in his life that it was no wonder he was always fooling around. It was probably the only way he could cope. It turns out that his dad died when Joel was a baby and cooking's never been his mum's forte, so the business went bust. Then, to make matters worse, his mum's not well either. She used to be a nurse but she hurt her back lifting a patient and hasn't been able to walk properly for over a year. Joel used to work two paper rounds to try and help out with the money but then the school complained because he was always tired, so his mum made him give up and now they're so behind with their rent that the landlord's threatening eviction.

'That's awful!' I was shocked. 'Can't social services help?'

'Oh yes,' laughed Joel. 'They've offered us a flat on the ninth floor in a block in Scarborough – great help!'

'I hate to interrupt this little tête-à-tête.' Ms Oliver was standing over us with a face like a carbuncle that was about to burst. 'You two have obviously finished the task, so perhaps you'd be good enough to share your ideas with the rest of the class. Alternatively, you can stay behind at lunch time and do the work you're supposed to have done in the lesson.'

Oh great! I'd already got one detention tonight with Mrs Twigg and our break this morning had been cancelled. Unless we could come up with something pronto, my lunch time sitting with Kameran's new clients would be in jeopardy too. Prison camp has nothing on this place.

But the good thing about working with someone as quick-thinking as Joel was that when it comes to winging it, he's an absolute eagle! So even though we'd done hardly any work, he stood at the front of the room and blagged it, selling our product – Fishtastic Feasts – till even penguins would be queuing up for seconds.

'You were amazing,' I said as we left the room at lunch time. 'Any time you want another reading, you can have one for free. Why don't you come to the back of the sports hall now? And if your mum wants me to come and do some healing on her, I'll do that too.'

Joel smiled. 'Cheers, but we'll be OK. Anyway, I've got to go and earn some money to pay off Eddy Proudfoot.'

I looked at him questioningly. 'Pay him off? What for?'

Joel raised his eyebrows, surprised that I didn't know. 'He's the one threatening to evict us – well, his mam is. She's our landlord.'

Oh no! This was too awful. Last night I'd had to witness Josiah Proudfoot bring about the downfall of Isaac Chapman and now I was hearing that, two hundred and fifty years on, history was repeating itself.

I had to do something – and I knew just the person to help me. But where was Quill when I needed him?

9

Typical – just when I was relying on Quill to help me out with the Joel situation, he didn't show up all week. Every time I did a reading I was waiting for the Arctic gale to hit, but – nothing! And it wasn't just that I wanted his advice on the Chapman v Proudfoot vendetta either – I needed him to put me out of my misery on the outcome of his unfortunate encounter with the dragoons. The last thing I'd seen he was hurtling down the face of a cliff without a bungee rope. I wanted to know if all the king's horses and all the king's men had managed to put Quill back together again, or if he really had been unbelievably macabre and taken me to witness his own death. I was starting to think I must have offended him – or maybe I'd imagined the whole thing? Either way, I couldn't get him out of my head.

But if Quill was noticeably absent, Kameran was working so hard at drumming up work for me that, by Friday, the queue for palm readings went halfway round the sports hall and on to the tennis courts.

'Whoa!' I said, as I came round the corner. 'There's no way I can do this many readings in one lunch time.'

Kameran shook his head in dismay. 'This is amazing. Hey – maybe I should think about a career in PR?'

'Well, right now, PR needs to stand for "people reorganisation", because I don't like letting people down. You'll have to start an appointments system.' Eeeew! You have no idea how much I hated saying that – it made me sound so institutionalised, like a health service or a bank.

'No problem,' he said. 'I'll see if I can cadge an appointment book from Mum and Dad's surgery.' See what I mean? 'So,' he went on, rubbing his hands together, 'would you be up for breaks and after school as well as lunch times?'

Boy, was he a hard taskmaster? But the truth was, Wanda and I desperately needed the money. Eva Proudfoot had a mouth the size of the Grand Canyon and her opinion of Wanda had gone round Whitby faster than the bubonic plague on turbo boost. Despite Teddy's best efforts to counteract Eva's badmouthing, Wanda's clients had almost dried up.

On the positive side, she hadn't packed our

bags yet (the jury was still out on whether that was down to having Mushka to look after or the fact that Teddy seemed to be a permanent feature in the kitchen), but she'd now resorted to her second favourite way of coping with disappointment – baking. We had so much food in the cupboard, she could have set up shop as a patisserie and made more money than she had ever done as a psychic. Even Teddy, with his fisherman-sized appetite, was having trouble eating his way through the scones, flapjacks, muffins and pies Wanda was producing.

That morning I'd taken a bag into school to give to Joel – I knew it would hardly pay the rent for him but I hoped it might ease their situation a little.

He eyed it warily. 'We're not a charity case, you know.'

'Listen,' I said, 'there've been times when I've begged on the street corner, not knowing where the next meal was coming from. People helped me out; now I'm helping you out. When you and your mum get back on your feet, you can do the same for someone else. It's Karma.'

'Calmer than what?' he said, looking in the vague direction of the sea.

I looked at him, trying to work out whether or

not he was serious. 'Just take the food, Joel.' And he did.

By Friday afternoon, I was feeling thoroughly fed up. I'd started the week with two goals: the first was to try and help Joel and his mum and the second was to find out what had happened to Quill. I hadn't achieved either. But worse than that, I realised that I'd been spending so much time doing readings to try and earn money that I'd turned into the sort of person I really despised – a materialistic money-grabber. And, on top of all that, I'd totally lost sight of the fact that Kameran was spending all his time acting as my secretary and hardly any time pursuing the girl of his dreams. You see, this is what they mean when they say the love of money is the root of all evil. I'd sold my soul to capitalism and now my friends were suffering too.

When I'd finished the lunch time rush, I would really have liked to take some time to meditate and get back on track, but as it turned out that didn't happen. There were so many palms to read that Kameran and I went straight from the back of the sports hall to Geography. Amanpreet had saved me a seat and Kevin had saved one for Kameran just the other side of the aisle.

'Hurry up, you two,' Mr Spiggins spluttered as we shuffled into the lesson.

I wasn't sure why we had to hurry; it didn't look as though anyone was doing much work. There was a video on about hurricanes in the Caribbean but most people were chatting or doing their homework from other subjects. Amanpreet was busy scribbling in her sketchpad. I sat down next to her and got out my exercise book.

I was trying to make out where the video had been shot – and even if we'd been there at the time – when Kameran leaned across.

'It was sweet of you to give Joel that food.'

I shrugged. 'It was nothing.' I wasn't sure how much Kameran knew about Joel's situation, so I didn't want to give anything away.

Then Kevin leaned over too. 'You know, my dad was going to let them have the cottage you're living in.'

Oh great! Now not only was I exploiting school kids to line my own pockets, but I'd also contributed to putting a disabled single mother and her son out on the street! 'Are you saying that we've deprived them of somewhere to live?' I felt awful. What use was a bag of buns when we'd taken the roof from over their heads?

'Don't be daft!' Kevin whispered. 'Joel's mum couldn't manage the steps.'

Phew! But even so, I felt guilty that we were living rent-free while Joel and his mum were scratching about for money and could be homeless in a couple of days.

'Maybe,' I said to Kevin, 'I could have a word with your dad and get him to let us off the decorating for a while and I'll give some of the money I'm earning to Joel?'

Kameran smiled. 'That is so sweet of you. But between you and me, I think it'll take more than a few quid to help them out. I never used to believe in bad luck, but when you hear Joel's story . . .'

Kevin leaned over again. 'I reckon someone's stuck pins in their effigy. Believe me, some seriously weird things have happened to him and his family.'

I was intrigued. 'What sort of weird things?' This sounded like my sort of territory.

'Dhillon!' Mr Spiggins squawked. 'Stop talking and come out to the front.' See what I mean about him picking on the nice ones. Did he yell at anyone else to stop talking? I don't think so! 'Perhaps you'd like to enlighten us as to the weather conditions that lead to hurricanes – you seem to know so much about them that you don't need to watch the video.'

Oooo! I had an urge to put up my hand and shout: me sir, me sir! I'd lived through so many hurricanes, I could probably teach him a thing or two about the weather conditions.

Kameran stood up to go to the front, but as his chair scraped back, it was as though the hurricane had somehow leaped out of the TV screen and ripped its way across the classroom. There was a violent *whoosh* and books and worksheets were whisked up into a spiral of paper swirling round and round in the middle of the room. Then some heavier things started to go too: jumpers were lifted off the backs of chairs and carried upwards, flapping their sleeves like big ghostly birds. Uh oh! As soon as the word *ghostly* came into my mind, I realised that this was starting to look horribly familiar. My heart sank. As much as I'd wanted to contact Quill all week, the last thing I needed was him paying a visit during class.

I started looking round the room for any sign of him but I couldn't see anything. Not that I would have noticed him with everyone jumping up and down and standing on chairs trying to retrieve their belongings. Pretty soon, anything that could be moved was being whipped up into the air; not just books and clothing but the tables were starting to rock backwards and forwards too. Some people were laughing, others were starting to get scared, but when Mr Spiggins's toupee was lifted right off his head and swept upwards, the whole room collapsed into hysterical whooping and shouting.

'Silence! Silence!' he shrieked, leaping up and down like a boiled egg on a trampoline. 'Whoever's responsible will own up immediately or you'll all be in detention! Come on, out with it! I know someone's got a fan in here somewhere. You.' He pointed at Kameran.

'Me?' Kameran looked aghast. 'Why would I bring a fan into school? And,' he held out his arms, 'where exactly am I supposed to have hidden it?'

'Well, you can shut that window for a start,' Mr Spiggins snapped.

I'd only known Kameran a couple of weeks but in that time, I'd never seen him looking so annoyed. He slammed the window shut and, weirdly enough, the wind dropped immediately. Hmph! I'd been convinced it was Quill who'd whipped up the whirlwind, but maybe I'd been wrong. All the books and papers fluttered back to the ground, the tables stopped rocking and gradually people gathered up their things and sat down again. The only thing left above desk level was Mr Spiggins's hairpiece which was hanging, like a dead rat, from the end of the fluorescent light fitting.

'Settle down now,' he spluttered, going as red as an overripe tomato. 'And you, Dobson, go and fetch the caretaker and tell him to bring his stepladder.'

'Nice of him to apologise,' Kameran muttered as we sat down.

I was just about to say something when I noticed that my exercise book hadn't moved; it was just where it had been before the temporary tornado. So I *had* been right all along. There was no way an ordinary wind would have left one book on the desk and sent all the others up to the roof. It must have been Quill! A momentary flutter of excitement shot through me. I did another quick glance round the room but I couldn't see him. Then I looked down at my book. The page was open at the centrefold and there, in beautiful copperplate handwriting, were the words:

*Meet me at the turnpike on
York Road after school*

I snapped it shut quickly. I didn't want anyone else seeing it. I glanced sideways and was relieved to see Amanpreet busily drawing a caricature of Mr Spiggins in her sketchbook but, too late – Kameran was looking directly at my book.

'Did you write that?' he asked. 'Wow, I didn't know you could do calligraphy. I can get you some work doing that too, if you like.'

'Actually, a friend of mine wrote it,' I said, trying to sound nonchalant.

'Let's have a look. Where'd she learn to write like that?'

I held my hand over the closed book so that he couldn't see it again.

'I'm not sure,' I said, hesitantly. But, actually, that was a good question; it had never occurred to me that Quill could read and write, let alone produce beautiful lettering like that. 'Actually, it's a he, not a she.'

'Oh,' Kameran looked surprised. He went quiet for a moment and then said, 'It must be someone you've met here, or else he wouldn't be able to write in your Geography book. Is it someone I know?'

'No. No one you've met.' I was on dodgy ground and wanted to change the subject as quickly as possible.

Then – saved by the permafrost! The temperature in the classroom plummeted to subzero. I wasn't sure whether Quill's arrival was going to make things better or worse, but it certainly got Kameran off my case. Suddenly everyone was shivering and rushing for their jumpers while Mr Spiggins rubbed his naked head.

'I w-w-will not t-t-tolerate this,' he said through chattering teeth. 'It's w-w-one thing to br-br-bring a f-f-fan to lessons, but it's m-m-much more s-s-serious when people start m-m-messing with the h-h-heating. I will not s-s-say this again – whoever's r-r-responsible, own up now.'

My conscience was telling me that I really ought to own up. Even though, strictly speaking, it wasn't me who'd messed with the heating, I was sort of responsible for bringing Quill on to this astral plane. I just wasn't sure my explanation would cut it.

Just then, the unmistakable voice of Quill sounded right in front of me. 'Come with me now.'

As my eyes did a quick circumnavigation of the room, he began to materialise, sitting on my desk, his legs swinging into the aisle. Oh great! This was all I needed. How did he think I was going to be able to communicate with him in front of an entire class of students – not to mention Mr Spiggins, whose mind was not only closed, it was five-lever deadlocked!

' 'Tis important that you come this minute,' he said urgently.

Like I can just walk out of a lesson, mid-afternoon! Hadn't he learned anything by hanging around for a quarter of a millennium? But I couldn't say that. Instead I opened my exercise book, just enough that I could write a couple of words but not enough that Amanpreet or Kameran could see.

Can't right now, I wrote.

'I need thee to come now.'

I'm in the middle of class, I scribbled – in case it had escaped his notice.

With that, he jumped down from my desk, tipped his head back and blew upwards towards the light. Mr Spiggins' wig fluttered where it was hanging on the edge of the fluorescent tube. Very gently, the white tube began swaying back and forth and Mr Spiggins' toupee gradually slid towards the end.

'I've h-h-had enough of this!' Mr Spiggins was shivering uncontrollably. 'You've had your f-f-fun. I'm sending f-f-for the h-h-head!'

The whole class was looking upwards as the wig fell off the light fitting and began tumbling downwards. I watched Quill take a deep breath then give one almighty puff, sending it wafting its way towards the door. At that moment Kevin arrived back with Charlie the caretaker. As they came through the door, the toupee was flapping its way across the room like an enormous hairy bat.

'What the—?' Kevin ducked down.

'Aaaagggh!' Charlie screamed and dropped the ladder.

Quill continued blowing the hairpiece out of the door until it hit Charlie in the face.

'Help me! Help me!' he yelled as he tried frantically to snatch the wig from across his eyes. He was tottering backwards across the corridor. 'Get it off me! Get it off – it's disgusting!' I watched in horror as he tripped over the ladder and fell backwards, hitting the fire alarm on the wall at the other side with his flailing arms and breaking the glass. Before you could say *twisted fire starter*, the whole college was starting to line up on the playing field.

I was relieved to see Charlie stand up. He was rubbing his knuckles where he'd hit the fire alarm, but other than that he seemed uninjured. As long as no one got hurt, I had to admit it was a stroke of genius on Quill's part.

I followed everyone out of the building, and as soon as the register had been taken and the fire engines had departed, people began filing back into college for last lesson.

'Follow me,' I heard Quill saying, so I dropped back from the rest of the group and followed him across the field towards the gate.

'Hey, Mimosa!' Kameran called out. 'Where're you going?'

Good question, I thought to myself.

'Keep walking,' Quill told me. ' 'Tis not far.'

But Kameran wasn't easily put off. 'Hold on a minute! Wait for me.'

I turned to face him and waved my arm, signalling for him to go back. As I crossed the threshold of the college grounds, Kameran, the college building and all the houses surrounding it seemed to fade from view. I was once again standing in the middle of nowhere, surrounded by rough grassland. There were a couple of farm buildings to my right and a woman was standing on the doorstep of a single-storey cottage with a heather-thatched roof. She had a tattered shawl clutched round her and heavy black boots on her feet. It was obviously winter because there were no leaves on the trees and the smell of wood smoke hung heavily in the air. In the distance, a man and what looked like a girl about my age were trudging along a road.

Again, I was struck by the quietness and tranquillity of the scene. A crow was cawing in a tree nearby but other than that, there was total silence.

'Come,' said Quill as he drifted across the grass in the direction of the man and girl.

'Where are we going?' I asked.

But before he could reply, Kameran's voice sounded from behind me.

'What the hell's happening? Where am I?'

Oh no! How on earth was I going to explain this?

10

'What is this trickery?'

I could see that Quill wasn't exactly over the moon about Kameran following us into the middle of the eighteenth century – but it wasn't what I'd had in mind either. And *I* wasn't exactly over the moon about Quill saying I'd tricked him.

I gave him one of my looks. 'I'm sorry,' I said, only I didn't feel remotely sorry; I felt furious. 'Are you suggesting that I tricked you into bringing Kameran along?'

Quill gave me an equally withering look. ' 'E be here, baint 'e?'

Never let it be said that I can't give as good as I get. 'Yes, he's certainly here, but let's see, who was leading the way? Oh yes, *you*! And who's the one who makes wigs float about the room and winds rage through schools and spring days feel like Alaskan winters? Hmmm, let me see . . . oh yes, it's you again! So don't *you* accuse *me* of trickery!'

Quill's eyes narrowed – I think he was trying to

look threatening but, to me, he looked even more smoulderingly gorgeous.

'You? Him?' Uh oh! I'd got so mad with Quill that I'd almost forgotten Kameran. He was looking pretty bewildered. 'Who *are* you talking to?'

Oh boy – how was I going to explain this one? 'You can see me, right?' I asked him.

'Durr! Course I can see you,' he replied.

'But you can't see him?' I pointed to Quill.

Kameran looked beyond Quill to the man walking along the road. 'I can see some old bloke wearing a brown smock thing.'

I shrugged. 'OK, I'll take that as a no.' I turned to Quill and pointed to Kameran. 'But you can see and hear *him*, right?'

'Aye – as clear as Ah can see thee. And tha canst be sure, 'tis not a happy sight,' Quill said, glaring at Kameran.

I looked from one to the other. This was going to require some very careful negotiation. 'Well, he can't go back on his own, so I'll have to go with him and—'

But before I'd finished speaking to Quill, Kameran interrupted. 'No way! I don't know what's going on, but I'm not going back. This is way more exciting than Spiggins' Geography lesson.'

119

I'm not normally one to do I-told-you-so, but I couldn't resist. 'You see, I told you history was more than just a load of dead people.'

Quill folded his arms and glared at Kameran. 'No good will come of this.'

'What's with all the negativity?' I asked Quill, but he turned his back on me, so I spoke to Kameran. 'OK, now you know how you've been really open-minded about my tarot readings and palmistry and stuff?' Kameran nodded. 'Well, if you stay, you're going to have to open your mind about three hundred and fifty-eight degrees further for this little beauty.' I kept it as light as I could, explaining all the mysterious happenings he'd witnessed at the cottage, at school and on the cliff in a bright and breezy voice. I hoped that if I said it as though it was the most natural thing in the world, he might not get totally freaked out. 'So there you go – Quill's just like you really, only this particular incarnation of his was a couple of centuries before your present one.'

I waited for his response but from the look on Kameran's face, I'd slightly misjudged the freak-out factor. He was standing stock-still with an expression that I've only ever seen on rabbits sitting in the middle of the highway as a ten-tonne truck was thundering towards them on full beam.

'Kameran?' I waved my hand in front of his face. 'Hey, once you get your head round it, it's no big deal.' I prodded his arm. 'Come on. Snap out of it.' But still there was nothing.

'Tha should nivver 'ave brought 'im,' Quill chastised.

'OK, enough of the period lingo. I know you're mad at me but I've got enough stress at the moment. And, anyway, you promised to talk nicely.'

Things were getting distinctly tetchy, but fortunately, at that point Kameran started to come round again. He blinked a couple of times and then spoke very slowly.

'I'm just going to assume that when I wake up, all this will have been some weird dream.'

I've never been one to miss an opportunity. 'Oooo – Wanda does dream interpretation. You could go to her and see what she makes of it,' I suggested.

Quill shook his head in exasperation. 'I have business to attend to. Now, art tha coming wi' me?'

I looked from Quill to Kameran. What a dilemma. I really really wanted to go with Quill but I didn't relish the thought of having to give

Kameran a running commentary on everything Quill said and did.

'Hang on a minute!' Kameran said, looking more animated than he had been a couple of minutes earlier. 'I can see something.' He pointed to my right-hand side, which was where Quill was standing.

'Some *thing*?' Quill said with disdain. 'I baint some *thing*.'

'Oh wow!' Kameran was leaping about the field. 'I heard that too!' Then added, 'Sorry, mate; didn't mean to offend you.' He came right up to Quill and began moving his hand in and out of Quill's chest and through to the other side. 'This is amazing. I mean, does that hurt?'

'Kameran!' I was shocked. 'Don't do that. He has feelings, you know. He is a living being – well, when I say *living* . . .'

Kameran cocked his head on one side and looked at me. 'You mean *living* as in *dead*?'

'Jeez! Don't be so peridontic,' I said.

'I think you mean *pedantic*,' Kameran corrected.

Quill had a face like a blizzard on the north face of K2.

'When tha's finished,' he said tersely, 'come wi' me.'

Before I knew what was happening we were standing in front of a five-barred gate across what was, at best, a muddy lane and, at worst, a long narrow bog. The man and girl were walking towards us.

The girl spoke nervously. 'What wil't be like, Faither?'

'Eh, lass, Ah've nivver bin further than Pickerin', let alone York.' The man shook his head dismally. ' 'Tis a sorry venture, if nowt else.'

'Will t'folk be grand?'

'Aye, but no grander than Squire Cholmley up at Abbey 'Ouse. Fret thissen not; tha's a clever lass and an honest one. Tell t'truth an' tha won't go far wrong.' He tweaked his daughter's cheek affectionately. 'Tha'll be all reet. Ah'll be there with thi.'

The girl hung her head and I thought she looked as though she was crying.

Suddenly, Quill passed through the gate till he was right in front of her. 'Oh, Jenna, my love. Do not weep.'

I watched as the girl walked straight through him, her eyes still downcast. Hold on a minute – *my love*? Hadn't he flirted with me only a few days ago and told me that I was a *comely maid*? And now

123

here he was, calling someone else his *love* – right under my nose! I felt my stomach tighten into a knot of irritation. Then I checked myself. What on earth was going on? How could I possibly be feeling jealous of someone who, if she were still alive, would be wrinklier than a pickled walnut?

As the father approached the gate, another man, who had been sitting on a log by the side of the road, stood up. Resting on a gnarled old stick, he opened the latch on the gate and limped forward, allowing the couple to pass through. The girl's father placed a coin in the old man's hand.

'Noo then, Tom,' the gatekeeper said, nodding his head in greeting. 'Tha's off ti t'Sessions, ist tha?'

'Aye,' the father replied.

' 'Tis a bad job,' the older man commented. 'God's speed an' may justice be done.'

The man and his daughter set off along the road and Quill again drifted forward, so that he was right in front of the girl. 'Jenna, 'tis me.'

But once more he was about as substantial as a bad smell and she walked through him without resistance. Quill spun round, his eyes following her as she and her father walked heavily along the road, her skirts hitched up and their boots caked with clay.

'Well, I think we can assume you know them,' I said, trying to keep the ring of jealousy out of my voice. 'But are you going to let us in on who they are?'

'Jenna and I were handfasted. We were to be wed next Midsummer's Eve,' Quill explained. Uh oh! There was that little knot in my stomach again. I really needed to get a grip on the situation. 'She's on her way to York Assizes to give testimony of good character.'

Phew! At least there was some good news. If she was going to be a character witness, at least that meant Quill had survived the fall – even though he must have been arrested for smuggling afterwards. But then an even worse thought came to me – all the stuff he'd been saying earlier about the Hanged Man! Surely he wasn't going to take me to see him being hanged – that would be even more horrible than seeing him falling down a cliff.

'Just hold on a minute,' I said to him. 'Let's make one thing clear – I don't really want to go to your trial unless there's a happy ending. So if Jenna's going to come up with the goods and get you off, then fine, but if not, I'm outta here.'

Quill looked at me as though I'd lost the plot. ' 'Tis not *my* trial. 'Tis Isaac's.'

'Isaac's?' I queried. 'So, what happened to ...' But even as the question left my lips, I knew the answer. 'Oh no! You're already dead, aren't you? Did you die when you fell down that cliff? You did, didn't you? How could you do this to me?'

Kameran was quick to come on my side. 'Aw, man! That is so out of order.'

Quill shrugged; his eyes still firmly focused on Jenna as she disappeared from view. ' 'Tis not about you, or me.'

'So why have you brought us here?' I asked – not unreasonably, I thought. 'I mean, it hardly warrants dragging me out of school, just so that you can have another gleg at your girlfriend.'

'Nay, that's not why I brought thee. But right now my heart is too full of love and sadness to speak. Pray, give me a minute.' Which, to be honest, I thought was a bit much. After all, he'd had two hundred and fifty years to get over her, so what good would another minute make?

I was just about to say so when we were all suddenly zoomed through time again and, the next thing I knew, we were standing on a balcony above a large room which was heaving with people. They were mostly men but there were one or two women who looked like rather tatty characters out of

Cinderella with their big skirts and lace collars. At the back, there were scruffier people and even a few children, all crammed in and all pushing and shoving and shouting, ''Ang 'im!' I fanned my hand in front of my nose – the smell of bodies and sweat was worse than the boys' changing rooms when the drains are blocked.

'Eeew! Where is this place?' I asked Quill.

'Assize court at York,' he replied, looking round distractedly.

'Look,' Kameran said, pointing down across the courtroom. 'There's that Jenna girl and her dad.'

At one end of the room was a panelled enclosure with several very grand chairs behind it and, directly in front of it, a table with a load of men in white wigs. Around the room were other panelled boxes; some had men sitting down while others were rammed full of people standing. I could see Jenna and her father squashed in at the back of one of these, and before I could say anything, we were all three of us standing next to them.

At that moment three men in long, white, flamboyantly flapping wigs entered the room. One was wearing scarlet robes while the others were in flowing black gowns. They made their way along the bench and sat on the chairs in the raised enclosure at the end of the room.

'Look, Faither,' whispered Jenna. 'Is that t'King?'

'Nay, lass. 'Tis t'judges. 'Tis them tha'll 'ave ti convince an' Ah daint mind admitting Ah'll not wager on a good outcome.' He shook his head sadly.

As I was looking round the courtroom, I glimpsed a couple of faces I recognised from the night on the cliff. One was in the scarlet and white livery of the dragoons and the other was the pug-eyed Riding Officer, Josiah Proudfoot, in the blue uniform of the Preventives. Standing at the far side of the court, partitioned from the onlookers, was Isaac Chapman. I was shocked to see how thin and ill he looked. His hands and feet were shackled and his clothes were dirty.

'What's happened to him?' I asked Quill.

'York Castle may be one of t'best prisons in t'land but 'tis not noted for its comfort by them as has to reside there.'

'Oh, prisons,' I said. 'Don't get me started!'

A hush fell over the proceedings and the judge in red turned to the dock where Isaac was standing.

'Isaac Chapman. You have heard testimony this morning of Riding Officer Proudfoot and Captain

Paggett of the King's Sixth Inniskilling Regiment of Dragoons, to the effect that you did wilfully murder one William Newton . . .'

It took me several seconds to realise that the judge was talking about Quill. I looked at him. 'William? Really?' I shook my head. 'Neh – stick with Quill. It suits you much better.' And then a second realisation hit me. 'Did he say *murder*?'

Quill nodded.

'But it wasn't murder; you fell.'

'Aye. Ah've telled thi all along, Ah need thi to right a wrong. And this is t'wrong.'

No problem – that was easily done. 'No, stop!' I called out. 'You've got it all wrong.' I pointed at Josiah Proudfoot and the solider. 'They shot at him. They did it. They caused his death. I was there. I saw it.'

But no one could hear me. The judge continued speaking to Isaac, 'Do you wish to address the court?'

He looked up. 'Aye, mi lord.'

'Where's his lawyer?' Kameran asked Quill urgently. 'Surely he's not going to defend *himself*?'

'Baint none,' Quill replied, without looking at Kameran – his gaze had hardly left Jenna since we came into court. 'Lawyers were for t'wealthy ti prosecute them as wronged 'em. T'accused man had to speak for himself.'

'You're kidding!' Kameran was shocked. Quill turned slowly to face him with a look that would've turned butter to stone. Kameran held up his hands in a gesture of capitulation. 'OK, OK, you're not kidding. But that's terrible.'

'Where was Amnesty International when you needed them?' I asked.

'Ssh!' Quill nodded towards the proceedings.

Isaac cleared his throat. 'What tha 'eard this morning wor a parcel of t'confoundedest lies,' he said, falteringly.

One of the judges in black leaned forward. 'Are you accusing officers of the King of lying?'

'Aye, mi lord. Ah am that. Ah'll own Ah 'ad a pistol wi' me but Ah nivver shot at no one.' Isaac went on to explain what had happened, but I was shocked because, to be honest, the judges didn't seem to be paying much attention – in fact, no one in court seemed to be paying much attention, they were all chatting amongst themselves.

Eventually the judge in red looked at Isaac. 'Do you have any persons to speak for you?'

'Aye, mi lord. Ah want ti call Jenna Nightingale ti tell of mi good character. She wor betrothed ti

William Newton an' would surely not speak well of 'is murderer.'

A hush descended as Jenna's father pushed her forward through the crowd. Her head was bowed as she stood in front of the judges. She spoke in a trembling voice.

'Ah've known Isaac three year or thereabouts, and Ah've allus found 'im ti be as kind an' thoughtful a friend ti Quill as—'

'Quill?' the third judge queried. 'Of whom do you speak, madam?'

For a minute I thought she was going to burst into tears but then she gathered herself and said, quietly, 'William Newton, sir. Only Ah calls 'im Quill.'

'You will address me as *mi Lud*,' he barked, dipping his quill into a pot of ink without even looking at her.

If there's one thing that gets right up my nose, it's arrogance – actually there's a few things that get up my nose, but arrogance is pretty near the top of the list.

'Hey!' I shouted out. 'You lot should be careful how you speak to people in this life, because you never know how you'll come back next time round. Just you show her some respect.'

Kameran leaned over and whispered, 'I don't think they can hear you.'

I raised an eyebrow. 'Well, maybe not on a *conscious* level.'

'Come on, girl. Speak up!' the red judge commanded.

I looked at Kameran and gave him a *you-win* shrug. 'OK, maybe not even on an unconscious level. But believe me, they will get their comeuppance.'

'Be hushed!' Quill snapped.

Jenna's bottom lip began to tremble and her eyes shot to her father. He nodded and smiled reassuringly.

She took a deep breath and went on. 'Isaac be a good man. 'E did teach Qui— William carpentry and William looked up ti 'im. 'E wor 'is closest friend in spite of t'age 'tween 'em. An' Isaac 'ad respect for Quill. 'E asked 'im ti be godfather ti 'is bairn when it wor born.' She looked up and stared Isaac in the face. 'Isaac Chapman baint no murderer. 'E be an honest, wholesome man an' Ah daint believe 'e killed William Newton – whoever it is as says otherwise.' Her eyes moved across the room to where Josiah Proudfoot and the dragoon were standing.

The judges continued writing, then the one in red spoke in a condescending tone to the courtroom. 'An honest and wholesome man who did persistently smuggle contraband goods into the country and rob the King of revenue.' He looked up, briefly. 'Thank you, Mistress Nightingale.'

'What a pig!' Kameran said.

'Hey, easy on pigs,' I said.

Next, Isaac called Mr Fleming, the pastor who ran a free school for the poor children of the town. The pastor told the court how Isaac was a God-fearing young man with a wife and child who had been living in the poorhouse since his arrest.

'Is that who taught you to read and write?' I asked Quill.

Without his eyes leaving the proceedings, Quill nodded. 'Ah wor his best pupil,' he said, modestly. ' 'Twas how I got my name – Quill.'

'Cool name,' Kameran commented.

The pastor then told them how Isaac had looked after his brother-in-law until Robert's transportation to Virginia in the Americas.

'Transportation!' I was horrified. 'But Robert couldn't defend himself. How could they transport him?'

' 'Twas because he was simple-minded he got

133

shown leniency,' Quill explained.

Oh boy – I was finding this whole trial thing extremely distressing. I know it must sound weird, but I'd got to know these people and I was feeling pretty depressed about it all.

'Do we have to stay any longer?' I asked. 'Can't we move forward a bit?'

The next thing I knew there was a whooshing sensation. The judges now had pieces of black cloth draped over their white wigs, and I was pretty sure that wasn't a good sign. The two judges in the black gowns seemed to be nodding off but the one in the red robes was peering solemnly at Isaac. Uh oh! I was getting a very bad feeling about this.

'Isaac Chapman, you stand convicted of the horrid and unnatural crime of murdering William Newton. This Court doth adjudge that you be taken back to the place from whence you came, and there to be fed on bread and water till Monday next, when you are to be taken to the Tyburn without Micklegate Bar, and there hanged by the neck until you are dead; and may God Almighty have mercy on your soul.'

The crowd gave a jubilant roar.

'No!' I called out, but no one took any notice. 'He's innocent!' I turned to Quill. 'This is terrible!

Take us back immediately. Why do you keep doing this?'

In front of us, Jenna gasped and fell against her father, sobbing.

'Baint finished yet,' Quill said.

Then one voice could be heard above all the others. A woman in a shabby bonnet, with a shawl wrapped tightly round her, pushed her way through the crowd to the dock and reached up to try and grab Isaac.

'A curse upon thi Isaac Chapman; and a curse upon all them as comes after thi.' She spat at Isaac.

'Eeew!' I recoiled.

The woman pointed a grubby finger in Isaac's face. 'Tha robbed my lad o' life afore 'e could see 'is own bairns grow; may t'devil deliver t'same fate ti thi an' all as comes after thi.'

Two men came forward and pulled Quill's mother away. Quill shook his head and sighed.

'Eh, mother. If only tha knew what tha'd done.'

Kameran looked shocked. 'Whoa! I can't believe this! Are you telling us that your mother put a curse on the Chapman family for all time and that's why Joel's having such a crap life?'

'Aye,' Quill said flatly.

'But . . .' You could almost see Kameran's mind

working. 'That means ... that's the reason Joel's dad died young.'

'Aye.'

'And unless this curse is lifted ...' All the colour drained from Kameran's face. '... Joel's going to die young too.'

'Aye.'

I must say, I think Quill sometimes takes the strong, silent thing a bit far.

'So what can we do? How do we lift the curse?' Kameran was almost pleading.

Quill nodded in my direction. 'That's for Mimosa to fathom.'

Oh great! No pressure, then.

11

I must remember to look up how this whole time-space continuum thing works. One minute we were standing in York Assize Court and the next, Kameran and I were back in front of the college.

'Bummer!' I said as I watched the last stragglers making their way back to lessons after the fire drill.

Kameran ran his hands through his hair and began walking backwards and forwards in an agitated way. 'I know. It's terrible. What are we going to do?'

I shrugged. 'Go back and finish Geography, I guess. I was hoping we'd been away long enough to have missed it.'

He stopped and stared at me. 'Are you for real? How can you even think of going back to college when Joel's life is in danger? We have to find a way of lifting that curse.'

Of course, Kameran hadn't seen Joel's tarot reading, which didn't show anything beyond his twenties. I, on the other hand, knew that that meant we had about five years to sort out the curse business, whereas we had only two days to save Joel and his mother from being thrown out of their home. I couldn't tell Kameran, though, because breaking a client's confidentiality is against all the rules. Then I remembered the words of the curse.

I pulled Kameran towards college. 'What did Quill's mother actually say to Isaac?'

Kameran shook his head. 'I dunno – something about dying before he could have children.'

'No, she didn't. She said that he'd robbed her son of life before he could see his own children *grow up*. Think about it – Isaac had a son but he was just a baby when Isaac was hanged. And Joel's dad had Joel . . .'

'Who was a baby when his dad died!' Kameran's face lit up. 'So as long as Joel doesn't have any kids, he'll be OK?'

I wasn't totally sure my interpretation was right, but at least it got Kameran to back off with the pressure of lifting the curse. 'Probably,' I agreed.

'Brilliant!' he said, breaking into a run. 'Come on; let's give him the good news.'

'Whoa!' I couldn't believe he could even think of such a thing. 'You can't go telling someone his family's been cursed and he can never have kids. Can you imagine the effect that would have on him?'

'Come along, you two – hurry up!' Miss Basham was patrolling the front of the college with a loudhailer.

Kameran's face dropped again. 'I hadn't thought of that. So what do we do?'

I shook my head. 'I'm not sure – but I think it's time to come clean with Wanda.'

As soon as the bell went I almost flew out of Geography. But halfway to the bike rack, Milly ran up and grabbed me by the arm.

'So, come on, tell all,' she probed. 'I saw you and Kameran sneaking off in the fire drill.'

Oh no! The last thing I needed right now was Milly getting all jealous of me.

'We weren't sneaking off.' I wasn't sure how I was going to explain what happened without telling a lie – which, as you know, I almost never do. 'I just went to look for something and Kameran followed – that's all.' Which was true – ish! 'But I really can't stop, I need to get home early tonight,' I added, hoping she might pick up on the urgency in my voice.

'Yeah, right! You don't get out of it that easily.'

She was grinning, but I suspected she was just putting on a brave face to hide her disappointment that I might be trying to get off with Kameran behind her back. 'You're going to meet him, aren't you?'

'No!' I said – which was absolutely one hundred per cent true.

But I wasn't helped when Kameran walked past. 'I'll ring you tonight and find out how you got on – you know . . .' He winked at me. '. . . About that thing we were discussing.'

Oh great! I don't think subtlety is Kameran's strong point.

'Wooooooo! And you honestly expect me to believe there's nothing going on, Cleopatra?' Milly said.

'Cleopatra?' I've been regressed to revisit most of my past lives but the Queen of Ancient Egypt hadn't cropped up once. I didn't know what she was talking about.

'Queen of de Nile! Get it: de Nile – denial?' she laughed, heading off in the opposite direction.

'Oh yes, very funny.'

When I got to the bike racks, I was annoyed to see that someone had ripped up the glittery windmills I'd attached to my handlebars. They were drooping over the basket in shreds. Great! First I'm told Joel's entire future rests on me lifting a curse, then my friend thinks I'm trying to get off with the boy she fancies, and now my bike's been vandalised. This was definitely not one of my better days. I looked round and saw Eddy Proudfoot walking down the driveway towards the gate. He turned round and gave me a sickening smirk. I didn't need intuition to know who the windmill-vandal was. I usually believe that no one's all bad or all good – even the nastiest person in the world has a speck of good in them. I wasn't so sure with Eddy Proudfoot, though. He and his mother were bullies and there was no way I was going to let them get away with it.

'Wanda!' I called as I burst through the door. 'You have got to help me sort out Eddy Proudfoot.'

I threw my jacket on to the hook in the hall and stormed into the kitchen, only to see Teddy lying on his back on the kitchen table with his eyes closed. Wanda was holding her Tibetan singing bowl about ten centimetres above his body, running the wooden striker round the rim so that it made a soft humming noise.

'Hi, sweetie,' she said, without stopping. 'Teddy's going over to Holland again tonight, so

I'm just cleansing his aura to give him the best possible chance of success.' She gave me a knowing look and smiled. 'And I don't think he's the only one around here who needs a bit of auric cleansing. It's not like you to take a turning down Rue de Revenge – what's going on for you, sweetie?'

'Nothing!' I snapped. OK – so my aura probably looked like a volcano on the point of eruption but I've never said I told the truth *all* the time, so I was claiming this as one of the exceptions. I really wanted to get Wanda on her own to fill her in on everything that had happened in the last week. I did feel horribly guilty about not telling her in the first place, but she'd been so preoccupied with Teddy that I'd have had more chance of getting an audience with Elvis.

I picked up Mushka, who had been curled up on the rocking-chair by the range, and plonked myself down to mull over fund-raising ideas for Joel and his mum while I waited for Wanda to finish.

Finally, Teddy stood up.

'I'll be back Sunday,' he said, kissing Wanda on the cheek. 'And I promise this'll be t'last run. I'll not engage in owt illegal again. But I'd be letting folk down if I dropped out at this stage o' t'game.'

Wanda smiled and went all gooey-eyed. I hoped

she wasn't going to invite him to stay longer.

'OK,' I said, eager for him to leave so that I could speak to Wanda. 'Have a good trip.'

'You know, your mam's a very wise woman,' he said to me, earnestly.

'Yeah, sure. Don't you have a tide to catch or something?'

'Sweetie!' Wanda was looking at me in this really weird way.

But Teddy was on a roll. 'Like your mam says, what goes around comes around.'

It was all I could do to stop myself groaning. When was he going to tell me something I didn't know!

'She's made me see t'error of my ways and I've decided, no more illegal booze runs. Nicking from t'government is still nicking, so I'll not be doing it again.' He grinned at Wanda, then added, 'Not that I won't miss t'money, though.'

'There's more to life than money,' Wanda purred.

Humph! Not if you're Joel Chapman, I thought. And then I had a stroke of genius. 'Hey, Teddy, do you make a lot of money on these smuggling runs?'

'Sweetie! What has got into you today?' Wanda was looking askance.

But Teddy seemed unperturbed. 'Aye, lass, I've made a fair bob or two in t'past. T'pubs and hotels are allus keen to get their hands on cheap booze.' He indicated the cottage with his head. 'And it's paid for this place over t'years.'

'And do you always work alone?' I persisted.

'Mostly,' he said, more cautiously. 'I've got a contact over at Saltwick as helps me unload but . . .'

'What about an apprentice? Just think how much more you could do if there were two of you. They always say two are better than one.'

All Wanda's good work on Teddy's aura was in danger of going out of the window as his face darkened. 'Nay, I know you young folk's allus after a bit of extra pocket money, but I couldn't let you . . .'

Holy Karoly! He thought I was after a job for myself! As if one trip across the North Sea with Teddy hadn't put me off boats for life. 'Not me!' I gave Wanda a quick rundown on the whole Evil Eva and Eddie Proudfoot eviction saga. 'And Joel is almost sixteen,' I pleaded. Then looked to Wanda and added by way of explanation, 'He's a Virgo; September the second with Leo in the ascendant.'

Wanda nodded thoughtfully. 'Interesting.' I could see she was softening.

Unlike Teddy. 'Nay – I don't care if 'e's got Lenny the Lion in the bloomin' attic. Joel's never been to sea before and 'e'd be a liability.' He was pacing the hall looking distinctly agitated. 'I've known Kathy Chapman since schooldays – long before her Jack died. She's got enough on her plate at the minute; t'last thing she needs is that lad of hers ending up in a young offenders institution – or worse!'

I held up my hands to stop Teddy continuing on such a negative note. 'Hey – don't even put that out to the Universe.'

Wanda nodded. 'Mimosa's right, Ted. You can only think one thought at a time, why make it a negative one? If you visualise things going wrong, they will, but if you visualise the run going smoothly, it'll be fine. And just look at it this way: by not taking Joel you're depriving him of the opportunity to earn good money and pay off their debts. So you could be sentencing your friend Kathy to eviction. The Universe works in mysterious ways, you know.' She looked at me and winked. 'Right, sweetie?'

'Absolutely.' I gave her a two-eyed wink back. 'And if you really want to make amends for doing something illegal, you could donate your share of the money to the Chapmans too.'

After some pretty heavyweight huffing and puffing, Teddy finally conceded. 'I'm not happy about it, though,' he warned. 'Not happy at all.'

'You're wonderful!' I gave him a hug. 'Believe me, with the way your aura was glowing earlier, you've got no worries. Now, I'll go and find Joel and tell him the good news.'

I breathed a sigh of relief. At least that was the immediate problem sorted; there was just the knotty little issue of the curse-lifting to work on now.

12

'A curse is just returning evil,' Wanda said, pressing oats and honey into a baking tray.

Teddy had left for Holland with Joel, and Wanda was distracting herself by indulging her baking habit again; we already had enough bread to feed half of Whitby, and now she'd moved on to the sweet stuff.

'And what's the only antidote to evil?' she went on, scraping the last of the flapjack mixture out of the bowl.

'Yes, I know – *love*.' It was almost midnight and I was exhausted – after all, with the trip back in time that afternoon, I'd managed to squeeze about thirty-six hours out of the last twenty-four.

'So there's your answer – the curse can only be lifted with love,' she said.

'But whose love and how does that work?' I mean, it was one thing for me to love Joel on a 'love thy neighbour' type of level but, no offence to Joel, if Wanda was expecting me to go beyond the bounds of your average platonic friendship, this curse could be hanging around for a long, long time.

She pulled open the door of the old cooking range, took out a tray of baklava and replaced it with the flapjacks. 'The Chapman family have to embrace the Proudfoots and show them love and forgiveness.'

I had a mental image of Joel embracing Eddy Proudfoot – eewww! Gross! Not for the first time I questioned what on earth had possessed a self-respecting girl like Milly to go out with him. I could only think that she'd been hypnotised or had had a temporary bout of insanity.

I picked a crumb of baklava off the table and sighed. 'If it's that easy, why hasn't the curse been lifted before now?'

Wanda looked at me as though I'd taken leave of my senses. 'Easy? Oh, sweetie, you should know that showing love and forgiveness is far from easy. Can you honestly say that Joel loves Eva's son?'

I almost choked on the baklava. 'Yeah, right! Like that's ever going to happen.'

'Well, there you have the problem – until he and his mother can do that, the curse is stuck to their family like superglue. They're the only ones who can lift it.'

How depressing was that? 'But there must be *something* I can do to help.'

'Well,' she said, eyeing the bread mountain that used to be the table. 'You can take Joel's mother some more food and offer to do a house cleansing. And, if she's up for it, give her some healing on her bad back.' Then as an afterthought she added, 'In fact, I might come with you.'

Which seemed like a good idea when Wanda suggested it, but in the harsh light of the following morning, she was definitely having second thoughts.

'I . . . don't know . . . how you . . . manage it . . . sweetie,' she gasped as she pushed the old mountain bike that Teddy had given her up towards Kathy Chapman's house. 'All . . . these . . . hills . . .'

'It's probably best if you don't talk,' I suggested, as her face turned a disturbing shade of puce.

Of course, it didn't help that there was quite a wind getting up – plus, Wanda hadn't exactly chosen the best clothing for a bike ride. She was wearing her multicoloured cheesecloth skirt under her purple velvet cloak, and when she wasn't trying to extract one or the other garment from the spokes of the wheels, her cape was billowing out behind her so that she looked like a cross between a galleon in full sail and a psychedelic Batwoman. If she'd been hoping to use this visit as a way of re-establishing her reputation and drumming up a few more clients, I wasn't sure she was going the right way about it.

'OK ... leave ...' she panted, as she leaned against the Chapmans' gatepost, '... the talking ...' A drop of sweat trickled down her forehead and plopped off the end of her nose, '... To me.'

To be honest, in her present state, even breathing seemed like a pretty tall order, but I've learned over the years not to argue. And, as it turned out, Kathy Chapman was amazingly compliant when we told her our mission. In fact, she was positively grateful. So much so that I called in reinforcements to help out and by lunch time, Milly, Amanpreet, Kameran and Kevin were all hard at work, clearing the garden, tidying Joel's room, dusting and vacuum-cleaning everywhere and, finally, washing down the paintwork with lemon and rosemary scented water. When the house was clean and tidy, I lit joss sticks in every room while Wanda went round ringing her Burmese bell in all the corners and lighting white candles to get rid of all the negativity in the house. Then Wanda and I both gave Kathy a Reiki healing session while the others prepared some of the food we'd brought.

'This is absolutely amazing,' Kathy laughed, cutting herself a second slice of curd tart. 'I've got the landlord coming round tomorrow and I was dreading it – she's a right old boot! With Joel away I didn't think I'd have the strength to tidy the place up on my own and the last thing I wanted was to give her any more ammunition to kick us out. In fact, with the place looking this good, she might even be persuaded to let us stay on – at least until the house is sold.' She looked round and beamed. 'Even my back feels better. Who'd have thought it?'

'If there's one thing I've learned since I've known Mimosa, it's to expect the unexpected,' Kameran remarked, taking a piece of baklava.

Kathy smiled. 'Well, this was definitely unexpected – I'd have needed a crystal ball to have foreseen this.'

'Funny you should mention crystal balls . . .' Uh oh! I *knew* Wanda had had an ulterior motive when she'd offered to come with me to help Kathy. She reached into the pocket of her purple cape and extracted a velvet-covered box. 'I just happen to have one with me,' she said, pulling a pack of tarots from her other pocket. 'Or the cards – whichever floats your boat.'

'Oh my goodness!' Kathy said. 'Joel told me that Mimosa had read his tarot cards at school, but I've never had my fortune told. How exciting! I think I'll go for the crystal ball – it's more mystical, don't you think?'

'Wonderful choice,' Wanda purred, opening the box and unwrapping the piece of lint that protected the crystal ball. Then she gently placed it on its little tripod in front of Kathy.

I turned to the others. 'You lot will have to go into the kitchen, I'm afraid. This stuff's personal.'

Kathy waved her hand. 'No. Don't worry about that. After all, it's just a bit of fun, isn't it?'

I heard Wanda's sharp intake of breath but I gave her a slight kick under the table before she could say anything. Even though Wanda's psychic ability was distinctly suspect after the Eva Proudfoot debacle, I knew she certainly never thought of it as 'only a bit of fun'. Everything had gone really well so far; the last thing I wanted was for Wanda to go into one and spoil all our hard work.

'Ouch!' she said, glowering at me and bending down to rub her shin.

'Sorry, did I catch your leg?'

'Mimosa – sweetie!' Wanda narrowed her eyes as she spoke. 'Bring a candle over here, will you?'

Then she addressed the others. 'And the curtains will need to be drawn.'

. She sounded a bit terse so I had all my fingers crossed that she didn't blow it.

I knew from watching Wanda at sittings that she liked to have a candle nearby, although not so close that the light reflected in the crystal, so I placed one of the white candles that we'd brought with us at the edge of the table. I've tried just about everything else, but scrying, as reading crystal balls and other glossy surfaces is called, has never really drawn me, so I was happy to sit back and watch.

When the room was dark, Milly and Amanpreet went across and sat on the old settee at the other end of the room with the boys. Kameran was resting his head on his hands and gazing intently towards the table where Wanda, Kathy and I were sitting. Milly and Amanpreet were looking distinctly dubious but Kevin had a grin like a half moon. I knew that if the adults hadn't been there, he'd have been rolling around on the floor with laughter.

Ignoring him, Wanda took a deep breath, cupped her hands around the ball and peered into it – for *ages*! Honestly, I've never known her take so long to see anything. I wasn't surprised that, after about twenty minutes, Kathy Chapman was wriggling in her chair. I must admit, even *my* back was starting to ache. I decided that if the Chapmans did get a reprieve from eviction, my next project would be to raise money to buy them something decent to sit on.

Milly and Amanpreet were nudging each other and making head movements towards the door and Kevin looked so bored, it was as though he'd had his brain removed. I was beginning to wonder if Wanda was dragging it out just to make it seem more dramatic. I caught Milly's eye and she pointed to her watch and then to the door. I nodded and put my little finger to my mouth and my thumb to my ear like a phone, to let her know that I'd ring her later. She and Amanpreet stood up and, with an audible sigh of relief, Kevin joined them. Kameran, however, remained rooted to the settee, firmly focused on what was going on (or not going on) at the table.

As the other three tiptoed towards the door, they waved goodbye. Kathy Chapman gave them the thumbs-up and mouthed, 'Thank you', then gave me a half-hearted smile. I must admit, I was in danger of nodding off myself, when Wanda gasped and reared back from the table.

'Oh my God! Look! Look, sweetie! Look into the glass!' she whimpered.

The colour drained from Kathy's face. 'What is it? What can you see?'

Milly and Amanpreet rushed back from the door and Kameran leaped up from the settee and came over to the table.

'What's happening?' Milly asked, looking terrified.

'Mimosa, sweetie.' Wanda's voice had dropped to an anxious whisper. 'See what you can see. I'd like a second opinion.'

'I don't suppose I'll be able to see anything; I've never done this before.' Flattered as I was that Wanda was asking my opinion, I wasn't sure I wanted to start my training in front of all my friends. Plus, I was starting to pick up on everyone's fear, which doesn't help anyone's powers of divination.

Oh boy! I needn't have worried about not being able to see anything. As I peered into the crystal, the normally clear quartz was swirling with thick dark grey clouds. It didn't require an expert scrier to know instantly that it was predicting something dreadful.

I nibbled my bottom lip nervously and looked to Wanda for some sort of guidance. 'What does it mean?'

She shook her head, more as a warning to me not to say too much than because she didn't know. 'Look closer.'

Again, I gazed into the crystal and, through the mist, I could just make out Kathy Chapman, dressed from head to toe in black and crying. She was holding a white flower to her lips, then she tossed it away. Was this some reference to when her husband had died? Again I looked to Wanda.

'An image to the left signifies a future event,' Wanda replied to my unspoken question.

Uh oh! I was getting a very bad feeling about this. The image of Kathy was standing to the left of the sphere, so there was no way this could be a scene from her past.

'And the size of the image tells you how far in the future,' Wanda went on. 'The bigger the vision, the sooner it's going to happen.'

I gave an involuntary shudder – Kathy's figure took up over half the globe! Whoever she was mourning in the crystal, it was going to happen pretty soon. I just hoped she'd got some long-lost ancient auntie who was going to pass over in the next few hours.

'Is someone going to tell me what's going on?' Kathy asked.

Neither Wanda nor I answered. I leaned forward again and continued to peer into the ball. Now I could see waves crashing against rocks. The scene looked very familiar, although I couldn't place it at first. And then I remembered – it was Saltwick Bay, the remote cove just round the headland where Teddy had dropped off Wanda and me when he first brought us to Whitby. It was also the place where he unloads the alcohol he brings over from Holland. Then into the picture came a boat. I could see Teddy on board – but he was alone. There was no sign of Joel.

As the images faded, a needle of icy dread ran down my spine. I could feel my heart beating faster and my breathing had almost stopped.

My eyes darted from Kathy to Wanda. I don't know who looked the more terrified.

Kathy stood up and backed away from the table. 'Stop it. You're starting to scare me.'

Then Wanda stood up as well. 'OK,' she said, in this ridiculously false voice, trying to sound calm. 'We'll go, then. Sorry to have bothered you. Do enjoy the rest of the bread and sweetmeats.'

'No!' I put out my hand to stop her packing up the crystal.

I didn't know what I was going to say to Kathy

but I knew I had a duty to tell her the truth. Wanda's eyes widened until I thought they'd fall out of their sockets. She began shaking her head wildly. Everyone else in the room was staring at me in terrified anticipation.

The vision I'd just seen in the crystal didn't add up with the reading I'd done for Joel a couple of weeks ago. I know a person's destiny can change depending on the choices they make, but I was sure Joel needed to have had a child before he died. How else would the Chapman line continue, if he didn't have a son to carry on the family name – and the family curse?

I turned to Joel's mum. 'I need to ask you some questions about Joel's dad and his family.'

'Just tell me what you saw.' Her voice was quavering. 'I know it was something awful.' She slumped on to the chair again and began crying. 'I didn't think it was possible to have any more bad luck. I don't think I can bear it.'

Milly and Amanpreet began to whimper as well – even Kevin wasn't grinning any more.

'Does Joel have any brothers?' I persisted. 'It's really important.'

Kathy shook her head. 'No – he's all I've got left.' Kameran, who'd been chewing his lip nervously, let out a sigh of relief. Kathy looked at me with wide eyes. 'Please don't tell me something's going to happen to him.'

'I don't know at the moment,' I told her. 'But I'll be honest with you – it doesn't look good.'

She let out a wail of despair, checked herself, then looked up eagerly. 'He's got a half-brother. Will that help? Jack was married before and he had a son called John. His ex-wife moved down south somewhere. Joel's never met them.' There was desperation in her voice. 'If it'll help I can try to trace them.'

My heart sank. I looked at Kameran and he closed his eyes as though trying to blot out reality. It was the news we'd both dreaded hearing. As long as there was an older brother to carry on the Chapman line, Joel could die at any time; he didn't have to have had children.

'I don't think it'll help,' I said quietly.

The atmosphere in the room was heavy. No one spoke. Then Kathy rubbed her hands up and down her arms. 'I'll put the heating on,' she said quietly. 'It's turned very cold in here.'

Oh great! I'd learned to recognise Quill's calling card by now. This was all I needed.

'Ah needs thi ti come wi' me.' His voice sounded from somewhere above my head.

Talk about lousy timing!

'Would you excuse me a minute,' I said to Kathy. 'I really need to go to the loo.'

'I'll come with you,' Kameran said – obviously picking up on the Quill factor too.

'What?' Milly and Amanpreet chorused.

Do you see what I mean about him being the most indiscreet person in the world?

Wanda shrugged. 'So what's the big deal? We've lived in places where a couple of dozen people have had to share one hole in the ground.'

'Eewwww!' Milly screwed up her face.

'Gross!' Amanpreet looked as though she might faint any second.

'A little too much information, thanks, Wanda.' I glared at her. OK – maybe Kameran isn't the most indiscreet person in the world, after all. 'I think Kameran meant he wanted to go *after* me – didn't you?' I said, pointedly looking at Kameran.

'I'll wait outside,' he said. At least he had the decency to make an apologetic grimace before he followed me out of the room.

As we went upstairs I could just hear Milly saying, 'I *knew* something was going on between those two!'

But right now, there were more pressing things

on my mind than Milly and Kameran's love life. Once upstairs, I pulled Kameran into the bathroom with me and locked the door.

'What do you think you're doing?' I asked, crossly.

'Whatever's happening to my friend, I want to be in on it,' he said in a hoarse whisper.

'No way!'

But before the conversation could continue, Quill materialised in front of us.

I tried to keep my voice low but I was pretty annoyed with him for wanting to take me back in time at such a crucial moment. 'How can you even think of wanting me to go back in time with you? Don't you know what's going to happen? Joel's going to die very soon if I don't do something.'

'Ah baint asking thi ti go back in time,' he said, dryly. 'Ah needs thi ti go forward, into t'future.' He raised an eyebrow and looked directly at me. ' 'Tis thy fault Joel Chapman's destiny's bin altered.'

Oh great – my day was getting better and better!

13

'My fault?' Nothing like dumping the responsibility on someone else to make the situation better, is there? 'How on earth can it be anything to do with me?' I protested.

'If tha'd just done tha job and not interfered, there wor every chance t'Chapmans and t'Proudfoots would've settled their dispute in t'near future,' Quill said, harshly. 'But, nay – tha 'ad ti try and fix things.'

I was furious. 'Whoa there, Blame Boy! There are two things I have to say to you – one, what do you mean, *my* job? And two; you have *got* to stop talking like that – you are really *really* hard to understand.'

Quill stood there smouldering. If he hadn't been looking so furious, he'd have been absolutely gorgeous. When he spoke again, his voice was more level. ' 'Twas your job to teach t'Chapmans and t'Proudfoots to respect each other.'

'Mimosa was doing that.' Kameran came to my defence.

But Quill wasn't going to let me off the hook. 'Aye, but she wasn't prepared to wait and let t'Universe unfold as it's meant to. She got a bee in her bonnet about sorting out Kathy Chapman's money problems.'

'I was only trying to help,' I pleaded.

'Baint your responsibility to sort out other folk's problems,' he went on. 'Folk have to solve their own problems – that's how they learn in this life. If you'd stuck to doing what you know, guiding 'em to make t'right decisions, then you could've shown Joel and Kathy how to forgive and break t'curse. Then their money problem would've sorted itself out.'

I was confused. 'But I'd read Joel's cards,' I reasoned. 'I'd seen that there was nothing beyond his twenties. I knew he was going to die prematurely and I couldn't just sit back and let that happen.'

Quill shook his head. 'Just because you can't see round t'next corner; it dun't mean there's nowt there.'

Uh oh! I was beginning to see where he was coming from. 'So are you telling me Joel *wasn't* going to die an early death?'

Quill shrugged. 'His future wor undecided. It

depended on t'choices he made.' He sighed. 'Now, though, thanks to you, 'tis very much decided.'

'So what can we do?' Kameran asked.

Quill looked at Kameran and shook his head. ' 'Tis not for you to do owt. 'Tis Mimosa as caused this, 'tis her as has to sort it.'

I stared down at my feet, avoiding Kameran's eye and trying hard not to give him an *I-told-you-so* look. Then the full impact of Quill's words hit me. He was looking at me and shaking his head. Boy – he had the most fabulous eyes! If I hadn't been feeling so guilty about poking my nose into Kathy and Joel's business, my tummy would've been doing back flips.

'Joel wor never meant to go to sea,' he said, flatly. 'By arranging for him to go to t'Low Countries, *you're* t'one as brought his death forward. Tha's got to try to make amends. Come.'

'Whoa!' I groaned as, once again, I was propelled through time and space. Although I'd found all this zooming about exciting at first, the novelty was starting to wear off. Even for someone who's as experienced as I am in most types of travel, it was a pretty weird sensation. Imagine being on a rollercoaster – you know the point when you lurch over the top and plummet downwards till it feels like you've left your tummy behind? Well, it's like that, only fifty-seven thousand times worse – with the added factor of total disorientation when you arrive! Not a good feeling, especially when you've just overdosed on Wanda's delicious rum babas.

I blinked, frantically trying to get my bearings. One minute I'd been pressed in between Kameran and a shelf full of toiletries in Kathy Chapman's bathroom; the next, I was standing on the edge of the cliff overlooking Saltwick Bay in the pitch dark – waiting for my stomach to catch up with me! There was a gale howling and, even though I knew Quill would be able to hear me on a telepathic level, it's hard to break the habit of shouting.

'OK – I know *where* we are, but *when* are we?' I bellowed. 'And how do we go about saving Joel?'

'Tha dunt learn, does tha?' Quill said. ' 'Tis not your job to save Joel. We're here to offer Joel a choice. 'Tis all anyone can do. Then 'tis up to t'individual whether or not they tek it.'

'Are you saying that, even if we find Joel, we can't save his life if he doesn't want us to?' I asked.

'Aye.'

'Wow – that's heavy!' I said, but what I was actually thinking was that *heavy* wasn't the word –

more like mind-blowingly, stomach-churningly horrendous beyond belief!

If what Quill was saying was true, by interfering in Joel's destiny I'd endangered his life. And now there was nothing I could do but hope that he made the right choice between staying and passing over.

'We have to find him,' I shouted above the wind. 'What time is it?'

' 'Tis two o'clock on t'morrow.' Quill's eyes never moved from staring out to sea.

'Shouldn't they be landing about now?'

'Have patience,' Quill replied. Then pointed out to sea. 'Look – yonder.'

I could hardly see a thing. Clouds were scudding across the slender crescent of the new moon, so there was almost no light to see what was going on. All I could make out was the wind whipping the waves into foaming white tops long before they crashed on to the rocks below us. The memory of Quill falling down the West Cliff was still fresh in my mind and I had no intention of following his example, so I stepped back from the edge.

'I can't see anything, can you?' I yelled in Quill's ear. Then a flash of light over to our left caught my eye. 'Look!' I cried.

166

The light was small but it was flashing on and off and, once again, we were shooting forwards until we were on a rocky outcrop at the edge of the beach. There was a man standing in front of us flashing a torch out to sea. He was wearing oilskins and the spray was pounding the rocks and splashing up, drenching him.

'Who is that?' I was still shouting above the gale force wind and the crashing of the waves.

Quill's eyes were scanning the ocean as he spoke. ' 'Tis t'man as helps Master Dobson unload t'contraband; Harry Hutton's his name.'

I was feeling impatient – we were supposed to be finding Joel, not standing on a windswept rock watching some modern-day smuggler in a sou'wester doing Morse code.

'Look, I know your sympathies are going to lie with the smuggling fraternity but don't you think you should be out there zipping about looking for Joel? If it's two o'clock on Sunday morning, we can't have much time.'

'There's allus time ti change t'future,' Quill remarked, holding my gaze till all my tetchiness disappeared and I thought my insides would go into meltdown. 'Every choice we mek in life changes t'future. 'Tis past as can't be altered.'

Oh boy – he was so gorgeous when he got all deep and meaningful. But I got the distinct impression that he wasn't referring to Joel this time – he was trying to tell me something about my life.

'So what are you saying?' I asked.

But before he could reply, he turned and pointed out to sea. 'Look!' he said softly. 'Follow t'beam of Harry Hutton's tinder.'

I screwed up my eyes and squinted into the night. I could just make out the white-painted bow of *Gwendora*, the small fishing coble Teddy had named after his mother and grandmother. It was riding the waves a few hundred metres out to sea and seemed to be heading straight for us. I strained my ears and could just make out the *put put* of the diesel engine as it neared the beach.

'Help!' I heard above the pounding of the waves.

'That be them,' Quill said. 'They be calling for help so they must already be in trouble.'

'Really? You think?' OK – it was a cheap shot and I'm not proud of it, but you have to remember the strain we were under out there. 'I'm sorry,' I said. 'But don't you think we should try to stop Teddy landing in this weather? If they weren't in trouble before, they will be if he comes in too close to these rocks.'

'Nay, 'tis what cobles were made for; landing in t'shallows and weathering storms,' Quill reassured me. Then added, ' 'Tis not Master Dobson's fault they be in danger.' Oh great, another dig at me.

At that point, Harry Hutton turned off his torch, climbed down from the rock where he'd been keeping watch and ran out to sea until he was thigh-deep in the water. As the *Gwendora* neared the land, I could see Teddy standing in the stern. He threw a rope to Harry and then jumped out into the shallow water.

Suddenly, we were next to them and I must admit, I was very grateful that we were a few hours in the future because there was no way you'd get me standing waist-deep in the freezing cold water if I could actually feel it.

Teddy was talking urgently – or rather, *shouting* urgently. 'T'lad's got no sea legs, 'Arry. He wor throwing up summat rotten and t'next thing I knows, 'e's gone. 'E must 'ave fallen ovverboard. Quick, get in an' give us an 'and to look for 'im afore I call out t'lifeboat an' land us all in it.'

' 'Ow long since 'e went ovver?' Harry called, as he pushed the coble back out to sea and jumped in next to Teddy.

'I can't be sure – a few minutes? Mebbe longer?'

169

Teddy started up the engine and, before you could say, 'Man overboard!' we were alongside them in the boat.

' 'E'll not last long in these temperatures,' Harry warned. 'We'd best radio t'coastguard.'

'Yes!' I shrieked. 'Call the coastguard. Call them now!' But, of course, they couldn't hear me.

'Nay.' Teddy shook his head.

'What!' I couldn't believe that Teddy wasn't going to radio for assistance. I looked at Quill in desperation. 'He can't do that! How selfish! He's so afraid of going to prison that he's going to risk Joel's life? Just wait till I tell Wanda what sort of a slimeball she's going out with this time!'

'If I go down,' Teddy continued, 'our Kevin'll be all right with me mam and dad, but if young Joel goes ti young offenders institute, 'e'd never 'ack it. And t'shame'd kill 'is mam. Nay, let's at least give 'im a chance. 'E wor wearing a life-jacket, so provided 'e doesn't do owt daft and try ti swim ti shore, 'e should be all right for a while yet.'

OK – so maybe I'd been a bit hasty in my judgement of Teddy and he did have Joel's best interests at heart.

'Where is Joel?' I asked Quill. 'Surely if you can whiz us backwards and forwards all over the last millennium, you can pinpoint exactly when and where he fell overboard.'

Quill looked anxiously out to sea. 'This baint like history, tha knows. Things that've 'appened are mapped out and set in stone, so it's easy to find where tha wants to go, but t'future's uncharted territory.'

Oh, great! Now he tells me!

'Come,' he said. We were off back through time again.

This time we found ourselves actually standing in the *Gwendora* right next to Joel. The little coble was rearing up and then crashing down so that even rushing about through time was a preferable sensation. Poor Joel had my full sympathy. He was hanging over the side and, to put it politely, very generously sharing his supper with the marine life of the North Sea.

'Not far, lad,' Teddy called to him. 'Soon as we get ti Saltwick, I'll put you out with t'cargo and 'Arry can get you 'ome. I'll not let you suffer any more than's necessary.'

But Joel didn't answer, he just groaned and hurled again.

'Too far back,' Quill said, zooming us forwards again.

The next thing I knew we were in the middle of the sea. It was really weird – I didn't feel wet or cold and yet I was bobbing up and down like a cork next to a bright orange buoy which was flashing its warning light, right in my eyes. It was OK for Quill – he was hovering just above the water. I was just about to ask him if I could drown, when another flashing light caught my eye.

'There . . . he is!' I called as I was tossed about like a rag-doll. 'Over there!'

Joel was floating face down in the water, his yellow life-jacket rising and falling as the wind continued to whip the waves higher and higher. I gnawed my bottom lip anxiously. It didn't look good and yet I was helpless to do anything.

'Do something!' I yelled at Quill. 'Get his face out of the water. He needs to breathe.'

'Baint owt I can do,' he said, matter of factly.

'Can't you blow him to safety or something?'

' 'Tis up to Joel now,' he said.

'What!' I couldn't believe what I was hearing. How could it be up to Joel when it was clear he was totally out of it?

This was awful. I couldn't just sit there and watch Joel die.

'Can't you appear to him or something?'

'Spirits can only be seen by them as wants to see.'

'Brilliant!' I said. 'So why did you bring me here if there's nothing we can do?'

'By, tha dunt do patience, dust tha?' he said. 'Trust!'

As he spoke, I saw Joel give a jolt and then a shudder. Phew! What a relief – he was coming round. Quill was right, I really do need to trust more.

'He's alive!' I cried, turning to Quill.

But Quill wasn't sharing my enthusiasm. He was staring beyond me, towards where Joel was floating in the water; an expression of intense concentration on his face. I followed his gaze to see Joel's whole body vibrating in the water. Then a white vapour seemed to be being drawn upwards from the crown of his head.

'What's going on?' I screamed. 'What's happening to him?'

' 'Tis his spirit,' Quill said, quietly.

'No – you can't let this happen,' I cried. 'Take me back further, then we can bring him round – or stop him falling in the water altogether. Or – take me back to Friday evening and I won't tell Teddy about Joel. I'll let him go to Holland on his own and

I won't get involved again – ever. I promise.'

Quill shook his head. 'Nay – what's done is done.'

14

I felt completely empty, as though all the energy had been drained from me. I've lived through earthquakes, been on the run from criminals and lost count of the number of times I've been arrested, but watching my friend pass over was probably the single most terrible thing that has ever happened to me. Knowing the pain and loss his mother and friends were going to feel was like a gaping wound in my heart – and that's before we even go down the whole *'it was my fault in the first place'* route.

I'm not usually given to crying, but I was pretty close at that point. 'You mean we're too late?' My voice was little more than a whisper.

'Nay, 'tis perfect time,' Quill said, the faintest trace of a smile at the corner of his mouth.

'Huh?' I was just about to accuse him of having a morbid sense of humour when the white vapour that had left Joel's body began to form into a shape that was unmistakably Joel. And he was looking round, bewildered.

'Hey up!' Joel's spirit gave a start when he saw Quill floating next to him. 'Who the heck are you? And where am I?'

'Break it to him gently,' I said to Quill.

But it was Joel who replied. 'Mimosa? What the heck's going on?' Then he looked down and saw himself floating face-down in the yellow life-jacket. 'Whoa! Please tell me that's not what I think it is.'

'Now, I know this is probably going to come as a bit of a shock,' I said, trying to put it in the kindest way I could. 'But I don't think things are as bad as you think they are.' Then I added, 'Well, not for *you* anyway – not any more.'

Quill drifted forwards and shook his head at me. 'Tha knows nowt!' he said, sighing deeply.

Joel was looking distinctly uneasy. 'OK, will someone explain who the guy in fancy dress is?' Then he stopped, looked from his lifeless body in the water to me and narrowed his eyes. 'Mimosa, you're not . . .'

'Absolutely not,' I reassured him. 'It's just you – and Quill, of course.' I inclined my head in Quill's direction. 'But, don't worry about him – he's been hanging around for centuries. It's a long story,' I added, seeing Joel's confused expression.

Above the noise of the squall, I could just make

out the chugging of an engine – and it was getting louder. I looked back towards Whitby and could see the lights of the *Gwendora* rising and falling with the waves. It was heading straight towards us. Typical! Teddy was too late to save Joel, which meant that he was going to blame himself for taking Joel to Holland and he'd be devastated. This was just too dreadful – and all because I'd meant well and tried to help Joel out.

'We need to hurry,' Quill said.

'What's the point?' I asked. 'You said yourself, you can't change the past. And Joel's already passed over. It's too late.'

Again he shook his head at me as though in despair, then turned to Joel. 'Tha time's not come yet, Joel. Tha must go back and finish what tha came to do.'

'You mean I have a choice?' Joel asked.

'Aye,' Quill said, pointedly looking in my direction. 'Tha's allus got a choice. Canst tha recall what tha wor thinking when tha wor in t'ocean?'

Joel's spirit closed his eyes and thought back. 'I remember thinking it was blooming cold in the water.'

'Tell me about it,' I said. 'I'm not even here and I'm shivering.'

'And,' Joel went on, 'how sick I felt and how tired I was of all the hassle with working and trying to earn enough money for mum and me. And . . .' He opened his eyes and smiled. '. . . and how I wished it would all end!' He beamed and, even though he was barely visible in the dark, I could see the cheeky Joel I knew from college. 'That's it – I wished it would all end!'

'And how dust tha feel now?' Quill probed.

'Well, I don't deny, I've felt better,' Joel joked. 'But I'd rather be chucking up than dead, any day!'

With that, Joel's features became less defined and his limbs merged until there was once again a shapeless vapour hovering above the limp form of his body.

'What's happening?' I asked Quill, urgently.

'He's made his choice,' he said, softly. ' 'Tweren't his time.'

And then I remembered the curse.

'No – wait!' I screamed as Joel's spirit began to pour back into the lifeless body in the water. 'You have to love Eddy Proudfoot if you want carry on living till you're old.' Oh no – this was awful. What if Joel had been through all that and I hadn't passed on the message in time? What if I hadn't lifted the curse and he was going to die for real in a few years' time? 'Embrace the Proudfoots!' I yelled.

Suddenly, the Joel in the life-jacket spluttered, raised his head out of the water and gulped in air with a loud gasp.

'Help!' he spluttered, raising one limp arm above his head and waving it feebly.

Quill and I watched as the *Gwendora*'s engines went silent and Teddy and Harry Hutton leaned over the side and pulled Joel on board.

'What kept you?' Joel coughed as he smiled up from the bottom of the boat.

I turned to Quill. 'Do you think he heard me? Is the curse lifted?'

Quill shrugged. 'Tha's done tha best. 'Tis up to Joel now.'

'What! Is that it?' I was in shock. After all that he was fobbing me off with some pathetic platitude about doing my best. I wanted – no, *needed* – answers. I don't think it was unreasonable to expect a little glimpse into the future to reassure me that after all that stress and rushing about through time, Joel was going to be OK; that it hadn't all been in vain.

But Quill simply looked at me, gave a sigh, then said, 'Best get thi back.'

And before I had time to argue, I was stumbling

out from behind Kathy Chapman's shower curtain.

'How'd it go?' Kameran leaped up from where he'd been sitting on the toilet lid.

I was in no mood for him to start questioning me on the events of tomorrow morning. 'You could at least have waited outside the door,' I snapped. 'What if someone thought we were in here together?'

He looked at me with a pained expression. 'Well, if you'd been away longer than about five seconds, it might have mattered. As it was, I'd only just plonked my bum down, when you were back again.'

'Really? Wow!' That would explain why I had such a head-rush. But this was no time to start pondering the effects of quantum physics. I began shooing him out of the door. 'Seriously, wait outside. I'll flush the loo, then I'll go downstairs and then *you* can come in and flush it.' Kameran was looking at me as though I'd just slipped into Cantonese back-slang. 'So that it doesn't look as though we've been up to anything dodgy,' I explained. You can tell he wasn't someone who was used to having to cover his tracks. 'I'll tell you everything tomorrow,' I added to try and placate him.

When I entered the living room, Kathy and Wanda were both staring at the crystal ball in silence.

'I've just had a thought,' I said to Kathy, as nonchalantly as I could. 'Why don't you give Joel a ring on his mobile and suggest that he finds a Dutch health food shop. He could get some Cocculus tablets and an acupressure band for his wrist. They're both brilliant for seasickness.'

I'd told Joel how to break the curse (at least, I hoped I'd been in time), and now I was trying to minimise the chances of him actually getting seasick and falling out of the boat in the first place. Wanda eyed me suspiciously, as if she knew I'd been up to something.

Kathy shook her head. 'We can't afford a mobile, love. Still, it was a nice thought. But Wanda's had another vision and it looks as though everything's going to be all right after all.'

I glared at Wanda suspiciously. 'Has she?' I asked. 'Well, then, there's nothing to worry about, is there?' I gave Wanda one of my looks and said, as meaningfully as I could without making it too obvious, 'But, just to be on the safe side, Wanda, why don't you phone Teddy and suggest they both take some seasickness remedy before they set off back?'

Wanda flapped her hand dismissively. 'What! Tell a fisherman to take seasickness tab—'

I narrowed my eyes. In fact, if I'd glared at her any more intently, I think I'd have burned a hole right through her. Hallelujah – she seemed to have got the hint.

'Oh yes, good idea, sweetie,' she said, picking up our mobile and pressing Teddy's number on speed dial.

I let out a sigh of relief and did a mental checklist to make sure I'd covered every possible angle. OK – so Quill had told me it was up to Joel now, but I was determined not to leave anything to chance if I could help it. Unfortunately, Quill or Life or the Universe was equally determined to make me butt out. Wanda flipped shut the phone.

'Switched off,' she announced. 'Still, not to worry – a bit of seasickness never killed anyone, did it?'

Sometimes I despair of my mother.

That evening Kameran asked me to go to the pictures with him and the rest of the gang but I wasn't in the mood. I just wanted to get through the night and satisfy myself that Joel got back OK.

It was some consolation that Kathy Chapman seemed to have been placated by Wanda's bogus second vision – at least I didn't have to worry about her for the time being. And Wanda was so on a high that she'd actually *had* the first vision that she was celebrating with another baking fest – and a bottle of dandelion wine from the deli up the road.

I went up to my room and stared out across the harbour to the arch made out of whale's jawbones on the West Cliff. Where was Quill now? I wondered.

I took out my astrological tarots and began shuffling them idly in the hopes that the energy might induce him to come back and give me a quick glimpse into tomorrow.

As the cards slid easily through my fingers, one slipped out on to the windowsill. Typical, it was my old friend the Hanged Man again, dangling upside down by one leg from his gibbet. I sighed. If only Isaac Chapman had been hanged upside down by his leg instead of his neck, his family wouldn't be in the mess they were in now.

'If you're around anywhere, I wouldn't object to a bit of company,' I said into the emptiness of my room.

No reply! I put the cards away and flopped back on my bed. There was nothing left for me now but the one thing that Quill kept telling me I'm no good at – patience!

15

If you're anything like me, you'll be itching to know if this whole saga has a happy ending or not. Well, to put you out of your misery – ish!

The happy ending bit was that, even without the Cocculus and the acupressure band, Joel and Teddy landed safely (if a little queasily) in the small hours of Sunday morning. Teddy was as good as his word and after taking Joel on a tour of the Whitby hostelries touting their contraband, he handed over all the money they'd made to the Chapmans. By the time Eva Proudfoot had gone round to issue a 'Notice to Quit' that Sunday afternoon, Kathy and Joel were able to present her with not only a full complement of back rent but also an immaculate house.

Joel was full of it on the Monday morning in Food Technology.

'You should've seen Old Ma Proudfoot's face when Mam gave her the whole lot. It was like she'd lost a tenner and found two p. But, get this,' Joel went on. 'Me mam only went and invited her and her Eddy round to tea.'

'Really?' We were supposed to be looking at the nutritional value of a beefburger, but I was leaving all that to Joel. Ms Oliver had completely overruled my objection that it had no nutritional value to anyone other than earthworms – and they only benefited when the humans had died of heart attacks or mad cow disease.

Joel gave a coy grin. 'Well – it was my idea.'

'Wow, that's a bit of a turnaround.' I tried not to let out a squeal of relief. 'What brought that on?'

He shrugged. 'Dunno really. It happened when I went to Holland with Kev's dad. You know, I was sitting in that boat, chucking up for England, and I suddenly thought of my dad's Star Wars Collection.'

Did I mention that one of the things Joel had inherited from his dad (apart from ingrowing toenails and a family curse) was his love of all things Imperial? Well, I didn't know either, till Kameran mentioned it when they were tidying up the house and he sucked Jar Jar Binks into the vacuum cleaner.

Joel was squelching the minced beef in his hands (gross!). 'So there I was, leaning over the side of the boat, feeling like a pile of poo and thinking how fed up I was of being scared all the time.' He looked at me and made an apologetic face. 'I know it's not very manly to admit it, but it's true. I've spent most of my life being scared. Scared of being evicted, of not having any money, that I wouldn't be able to support my mum. And even,' he cleared his throat, 'that I might die young like my dad.' He straightened his shoulders again and patted the beef into rounds. 'And I started to feel really pissed off about it. Then, suddenly, it was like Yoda himself was speaking to me. This voice was saying to me, *Fear leads to anger; anger leads to hate; hate leads to suffering.*'

Whoa! I did not see that coming. Wanda always says the Universe will use whatever means necessary to get its point across. 'And it's true,' he went on. 'Fear really does lead to the Dark Side.'

'I know; I saw the film too,' I told him. 'Although it was dubbed into Romanian, so I think it probably lost something in translation.'

He gave me a weird look, then went on, 'And guess what?'

'Surprise me,' I said, keeping all my fingers and toes crossed that he was going to tell me that the Chapmans and the Proudfoots had become best buds overnight.

'Eddy Proudfoot's into Star Wars memorabilia like my dad was! He's got the limited edition Star Wars Monopoly set and he's going to bring it over tonight.'

Well, it might not have been the earthshattering embrace scenario I'd envisaged, with starburst fireworks in the background and a hundred-piece orchestra playing the victory march, but it was certainly a start.

'Wow – live long and prosper,' I said – and believe me, I meant it.

Joel looked up from the disgusting heap of meat he was mauling and shook his head. 'That's from Star *Trek*, not Star *Wars*. Don't you know anything?'

'Didn't I say something got lost in translation?' Honestly, some people are so ungrateful. 'Well, anyway – may the Force be with you!'

And, in fact, it seems as though the Force has been with Joel and Kathy ever since. So much has happened in the last month that it's hard to keep up sometimes.

Eva Proudfoot decided not to sell Kathy and Joel's place for the time being but put her own house on the market instead. She's negotiating to buy a small corner shop with a flat above, which could give a whole new meaning to the term *convenience* store. And, once the worry of losing her home was off her mind, Kathy's back improved so much that she was able to take on the post of practice nurse at Kameran's parents' surgery. She's got so much more energy now that she even found the time to trace and contact Joel's half-brother, John. It turns out that he's married and has moved back up north. He's now living in York and his wife's expecting twin daughters. Apparently it's the first time the first-born child of that particular branch of the Chapman family has been a girl for over two hundred years, so it looks like the curse might finally have been lifted. It would have been nice to have checked with Quill just to be sure, but do you think he'd put in an appearance since that night in the North Sea? No chance.

So, that's the happy endings for you. As for the rest of the story, you'll have to wait and see.

My career as a relationship guru floundered at the first hurdle. It seems that I'd got it completely wrong about Kameran and Milly. Milly had had her eye on Kevin for months – long before I even arrived in Whitby. Apparently, she only went out with Eddy to try and make Kevin jealous. So now she and Kevin are an item. And Joel has asked Amanpreet out too, which is so sweet.

The downside of all my interfering in the Chapmans' affairs was that Teddy realised he had much more in common with Kathy than he did with Wanda – oops! I thought Wanda was going to pack our bags and move on again, but then the guy who owns the deli tasted one of her vegetable samosas and she's found herself a nice little niche baking for him.

As for me, well, what can I say? I'm still doing readings and getting a steady flow of clients. Kameran's a great mate and we hang out together a lot of the time.

'You seem to have taken the news about Milly and Kevin incredibly well,' I remarked one evening when we'd gone for a walk up on the East Cliff by the ruins of the old abbey.

Kameran shrugged. 'What's not to take well?' he asked. 'I've known Milly since nursery and Kevin's my best mate. I think it's brilliant.'

'But I thought you fancied her?'

Kameran shook his head. 'Neh – don't know where you got that from.'

I was confused. 'But that first time I did you a reading, you said there was someone you really liked and you wanted to know if it was going anywhere. I thought it was Milly.'

He shook his head then turned away and looked out to sea. 'There was someone,' he said. 'But she just wanted to be friends.' I thought he looked a bit sad, but then he gave me a smile. 'And that's cool. Anyway, I really need to pee. Wait here a second.'

There are definite advantages to being a boy! I sat down on the grass to wait for Kameran while he ran back and disappeared behind one of the ruined abbey walls. I remembered when I'd been regressed back to my life as a barrow boy in the eighteen hundreds – so much easier than messing about with all those petticoats and pantaloons.

It was May and the sun was setting over the West Cliff, behind the town. Seagulls were crying and I closed my eyes to listen to the gentle lapping of the waves below. A sudden chill came over me and I shuddered. It was a still evening with no hint of a breeze but I hadn't seen Quill since the night Joel had chosen not to cross over, so it didn't occur to me that he could be up to his old tricks again. I pulled my cardigan round me and gave another shiver. And there he was!

'Well, hello, stranger,' I said. 'Where've you been hiding yourself?'

'I've come to tek my leave,' he said.

'Take your leaf?'

'My *leave*,' he said. 'I'm off.'

'Off?' I queried.

'Going!' he emphasised. 'By! Dust tha want it spelled out for thee?'

Whoa! Tetchy, or what? 'Are you trying to tell me you're going to pull away for good?'

'Aye,' he replied.

'So, I'll never see you again?'

'Aye.'

Oh no! This was dreadful. 'But we work so well together,' I protested. 'I think we could make a really cool couple.'

'I think you're forgetting summat,' Quill said, flatly. 'I'm dead!'

I looked straight into his gorgeously gooey eyes. 'And your point?'

'Listen, tha's got a good 'un, in yon Kameran. Tha could do a lot worse for thissen.'

Kameran? I could hardly believe my ears. I mean Kameran was great – I really liked him as a friend but . . . Uh oh! Hadn't he just told me that he fancied someone who only thought of him as a friend?

'Aye,' Quill replied, as though reading my mind. 'There's none so blind as them as dunt want to see. He thinks t'world o'you, tha knows.'

'Hey! Quill! How you doing, mate? I thought it'd turned a bit nippy.' It was Kameran, back from his call of nature.

I turned round to face him and felt myself blushing. Whoa! This was bizarre. In the two months that I'd known him, I'd always assumed that Kameran fancied Milly. I'd never even looked at him in romantic terms, but actually, now Quill came to mention it, he was rather gorgeous.

'So, what's happening?' Kameran went on. 'You're not going to whisk Mimosa away again, are you?'

'Nay. 'Tis time for me to cross over. I've done what needed doing.'

'Before you go, there's one thing that's been baffling me,' Kameran queried. 'If it was your mother who put the curse on the Chapman family, why wasn't the vendetta between the Newtons and the Chapmans? Mimosa's explained that Josiah Proudfoot was the Riding Officer who caught you, but he didn't put the hex on Isaac's family, did he?'

Wow – gorgeous *and* a genius! Why hadn't I thought of that?

Quill looked uncomfortable. ' 'Tis not summat I'm proud of, but Josiah Proudfoot wor my stepfather.'

'Whoa! You kept that quiet,' I said.

'Aye, my mam married him not long after my dad died, when I wor a lad. So it made it like a double betrayal when he turned on us. Not that it was intentional – he'd led t'dragoons there to arrest t'others what were going to land t'lugger at Upgang. 'Twas only 'cos Dusty Miller had got drunk and fallen asleep that me, Isaac and Robert were there at all. And my mam couldn't bear to think that her own husband would have a hand in her son's death, so she put t'blame on Isaac.'

'Man, that's heavy.' Kameran shook his head.

'What happened to Robert?' I asked.

'He worked as a slave on a tobacco plantation in the Virginias for ten year and then earned his freedom. 'E met a lass who wor a slave on t'same plantation and they started their own farm. Robert had two bairns, both lasses, and died of an abscess on his tooth when 'e wor fifty-one.'

I nodded. 'Well, at least he had some sort of life. But what about the others? What happened to Elizabeth and the baby?'

Quill smiled. 'Elizabeth died of consumption in t'poorhouse but Isaac's lad, Ruben, wor taken on as a houseboy when he wor ten. He married a flighty little kitchen-maid who did the dirty on him, leaving him with their baby son to bring up on his own.'

I gasped. 'But presumably he died before the child could grow up, so what happened to the baby?'

Quill shook his head and grinned. 'Nay – Ruben lived to see his grandchildren grow big and strong.'

I was confused again. 'But what about the curse?'

Quill shrugged. 'Like I told you – folk see what they want to see.'

'So are you saying there wasn't a curse?' Kameran asked.

Again Quill shrugged. 'Tragedy happens to all folks, it all depends what you focus on. Joel's family have passed down t'belief that they're unlucky through generations. But t'truth is, they've had as much luck as most. Aye, 'tis true, several menfolk have died early, but there's many as hasn't.'

'So, are you telling me that all that zooming about was completely pointless?' And it wasn't just the zooming about either – it was all the worry and stress that went with it.

'Nay – nowt's ever pointless – there's learnings in everything as happens to us. A curse is in the mind of the believer and it wor necessary for you to make Joel see the truth of his life. Like I said, Joel's future wor uncertain. He believed he wor going to die young and he probably would've done.'

'You mean like a self-fulfilling prophecy?' Kameran asked.

'Mebbe – who knows? All I know now is that Joel's future looks rosy. And 'tis time for me to go.'

Just as, that night at sea, Joel's spirit had become a shapeless vapour, so Quill's features now began to blur and lose their definition.

'Wait, wait!' I called. 'What about Jenna?' And, amazingly enough, I didn't feel the least bit jealous as I said her name.

I just caught the merest hint of a smile on Quill's fading lips. 'She's been waiting for me, these past two hundred and fifty year. Mek sure tha dunt wait that long to find happiness thissen.'

With that his spirit became a fine white vapour which began to spiral upwards. At that moment, a bright light appeared above us and Quill was drawn into the light. Kameran and I watched until there was no longer any trace of Quill and the light faded again.

'Are you OK?' Kameran asked.

I nodded. 'Actually, I am. I thought I'd be sad to see him go, but I'm fine.'

'You know what he said about there being learnings in everything?' he asked, gazing out to sea. 'What do you think your lesson has been in all this?'

I thought for a moment. Wow – there were so many! 'Well, I've learned not to try and fix things for other people – big time!' I laughed. 'And I suppose I've learned that I've got a gift and I should use it wisely. What about you?'

Kameran took a deep breath. 'I've learned to grab happiness while I can.' He slipped his hand in mine. 'Because even with a crystal ball, we never know what's round the corner.'

I felt a tingle of excitement in my tummy.

'Cool,' I smiled, leaving my hand where it was and giving Kameran's a little squeeze.

So there you have it! That's why I don't want to call this a happy ending – because I don't know whether the ending will be happy or not. All I know is that right now, this is a very happy beginning!

A note from the author

I was born and brought up in Yorkshire
and often went to Whitby as a child.
It's such an interesting and evocative place
and holds lots of memories for me, so when I
had the idea for Mimosa, I knew I wanted to set
the story in Whitby. Doing the research for a book
is one of the best parts for me and this gave
me the opportunity to go back and revisit
my childhood haunts. It was a real
nostalgia-fest. I loved it.

MAGENTA ORANGE

Echo Freer

Magenta Orange has the world at her feet. If she could just stop tripping over them.

Bright, sassy and massively accident prone, Magenta's seen as a jinx by her mates – and a disaster zone by the boy of her dreams. Blind to the longing looks of her best friend, Daniel, and the sweet nothings of school freak, Spud, she's set her sights on year 11 hottie, Adam Jordan – and she'll risk everything, even total humilitation, in her relentless pursuit of a date . . .

'A wicked, witty read – 5/5!' *Mizz* magazine

MAGENTA IN THE PINK

Echo Freer

Magenta Orange is back – and this time she's centre stage . . .

Magenta is desperate to star in the school production of Grease – she's always fancied being a Pink Lady – but chaos at the casting means she ends up stuck firmly behind the scenes. And it's not long before she's getting into trouble again – developing a crush on the leading man, accidentally sabotaging the scenery and trashing ex boyfriend Daniel's skateboard in a vain attempt to impress hunky bad boy Ryan. Now it's not just the set crashing around her ears, but all her dreams of super-stardom and snogging too . . .

BLAGGERS

Echo Freer

Mercedes Bent is trying to go straight – if only her family weren't so crooked . . .

Mercedes has carved herself a nice little niche at the Daphne Pincher Academy for Young Ladies, running a sweepstake and taking bets on anything that moves. The only fly in the ointment is her arch-rival, gangster's daughter Harley 'halitosis' Spinks. How come *she's* got the great work placement and Mercedes has ended up in a boring bank?

But things start to look up when Mercedes wangles a date with the bank's hottest young trainee, Zak – until she finds out that it's not just the Spinks gang who are into dodgy dealing; her own brothers are as crooked as a pair of corkscrews too! It's a safe bet that Mercedes will have to keep her family's illegal activities under wraps – if she's to have even an outside chance with the boy of her dreams . . .